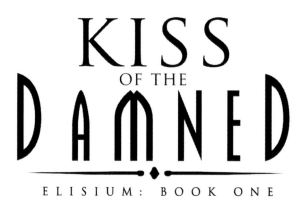

KISS
OF THE
DAMNED

ELISIUM: BOOK ONE

ELENA LAWSON

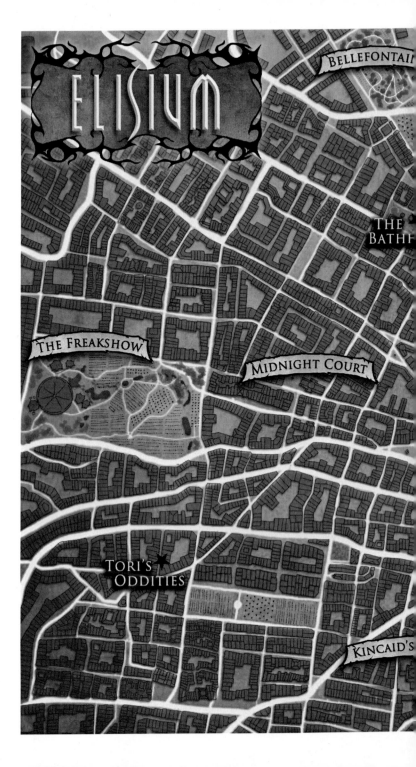

ELISIUM

BELLEFONTAI[NE]

THE
BATH[

THE FREAKSHOW

MIDNIGHT COURT

TORI'S
ODDITIES

KINCAID'S

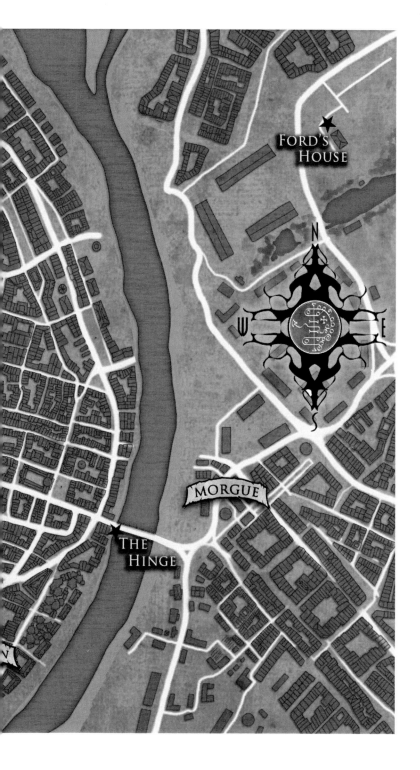

FORD'S
HOUSE

N

W   E

MORGUE

THE
HINGE

DEDICATION

For Ryan Reynolds
It never would have worked out between us.

W e stand outside the door to the room where they are keeping Ford's body. Me and the two officers with their drawn faces and downturned eyes. The woman moves to touch me, and I shrink back from her reaching hand, wrapping my arms protectively around my chest.

"Are you ready?" the female officer asks in a hushed tone as the male presses his palm to the door, awaiting my reply.

Beyond the rectangular window, awaits a sterile room. Clean tile floors and stainless-steel walls and humming fluorescent lights.

Little silver handled doors checker the back wall, and within them, dead people lie chilled on slabs of metal. But what draws my eye most is squatted at the middle of the space: a lumpy form covered loosely in a white sheet.

Ford.

"We just need you to ID the body and then we can leave," the older male officer says in a gruff, professionally-detached tone. I wonder how many bodies he's seen. How many loved ones he's watched cry over corpses.

"But I will warn you," he continues when I do not reply. "Due to the...*nature* of his injuries and how we found him—well, it isn't pretty."

"I understand," I say flatly, afraid of what other words might come out if I'm not careful. "I'm ready to see him now."

The officers share a look before they escort me into the room. A burst of prickling cold brushes over my bare arms, making my teeth clench. But that isn't the worst part.

The worst part is the smell.

It's faint. They've gone to painstaking lengths to ensure the cleanliness of this room for visits such as this. But I know the smell of death better than most ever could.

Panic lodges in my throat, and I clench my hands around my arms tighter, trying to force the horrid memories back into the dark places of my mind.

Ford said it was for my own good—the things he did to me.

He said he was protecting me. Keeping my fragile body alive by keeping me locked up tight. Severe combined immunodeficiency—they're fancy words for saying I am *weak*. I can't even stand up to the common cold and hope to survive.

The officers' footsteps clack and echo against the tile. My only-worn-once sneakers squeak, damp from the puddle I stepped in on the sidewalk outside.

The male officer waits for my nod before drawing back the white sheet to reveal the grotesquerie that is Ford.

His swollen face looks near bursting, tinged in hues of blue, red, and green with patches that seem bleached of all color. He is nearly unrecognizable.

His hair, always meticulously combed back is disheveled, revealing more gray strands than I remember. And his nose, broken and crooked, looks strange. Worse than all the rest is the injury in the top right portion of his skull. A mean indentation, ringed in puckered and mutilated flesh.

"It's him," I croak, eyes welling even though my chest is light as air.

It's really him.

The female officer rubs a hand over my back, and I try my best not to flinch away, merely stiffening at the contact.

"You did great, honey."

The other officer re-covers Ford's face, and I burst into a sob, shuddering at the intensity of the feeling flowing through my veins. Swelling like a geyser beneath my skin.

A grin I can't help spreads wide on my lips.

I am free.

2

When the officers came that morning, I'd still been asleep. The sound of the door- bell echoing through the house might as well have been a gunshot in the dark of my shuttered room.

No one came to our house. Not ever.

I hadn't even known what the doorbell sounded like.

It was almost…*cheery*. So incredibly divergent from what lay within. Ford's house was a modern fortress complete with bars and security shutters on the windows and a panic room in the basement right next to the dead room.

I wait in the safe warmth of my bed, thinking I imagined the sound, but then it comes again, this time followed by a series of thumps on the door.

"Police," a man's voice shouts. "Anybody home?"

Police?

Hope swells for an instant beneath my rib cage before I quash it, settling myself with several deep breaths as I shakily rise from my bed.

I tried to escape before. Lots of times. Twice, I had gotten to the police, and twice they hadn't believed me. Ford always had a better story for them—a more believable one.

That I was certifiably insane was his favorite go-to. The bastard even had the forged paperwork to prove it. And the more I ranted and raved that he was the crazy one, that he was the one who was insane, the more they believed him.

People believe what is easier. They believe what they want to. The truth is an inconvenience they can't afford.

"Police!" comes a second shout.

Think, Paige. What should you do?

Ford isn't rushing to answer the door. In fact, I can't hear him or anything else at all in the house. Which means he didn't return home last night. There's no way he would've hesitated for even a second to get these people away from the house.

With trembling fingers, I change into jeans and a tank-top to the sound of more thuds at the front door. I drag a brush through my brightly hued hair and pull on a pair of socks, hopping out the door in my haste.

Halfway to the entrance though, I pause, heart in my throat.

I haven't taken my pills yet. Ford always gives me my pills in the morning, and if there is any risk of running into other people, he always gives me a double dose. They're in his room, but there's no way for me to retrieve them. Ford's door is reinforced steel with a combination lock, not unlike a door you might find on the safe in a bank's vault.

"Hello?" A female voice calls this time. "Anybody home?"

Swallowing past the lump in my throat, I pad to the entryway, peering at the screen in the hall. It shows the view from the exterior cameras.

The one positioned over the front door shows two police officers dressed in dark colors, weaponry strapped across their waists, hands on hips.

They aren't Nephilim. It's easy to tell the supernaturals apart from us naturals.

Though I've had no face to face experience with the other beings now sharing our world, Ford made certain I had some idea what they looked like. He also took steps to make certain I'd never go near one for as long as I lived.

Nephilim are unnatural, he would growl during our lessons. *Abominations. But their wickedness is* nothing *compared to the Diablim.*

I glance toward the door only a few meters away. It too is strong and sports three different types of locks. I could open it. Ford didn't have to keep it sealed anymore, not since he installed the new hardware on my ankle eight years ago.

Though without my pills…

I tap the intercom button beside the wide panel of screens and lick dry lips. "Um, Mr. Ford isn't home right now." I speak into the receiver. "Could you… could you come back later?"

I chide myself for my weakness. For my unwillingness to provoke Ford's wrath in trying to escape a third time. It won't work. And it isn't worth getting the hose again. Or the chair.

The female officer scans the exterior wall for the intercom and bends to speak into it. "Paige St. Clare?"

My finger freezes over the button, trying to make sense of what's happening. How do they know my name? What would they want with *me*?

Hesitantly, I thumb the button again. "Yes?"

"Could you come to the door? We need to speak with you."

I release the button and back away from the wall, frantically glancing between the door and the intercom.

Why?

I want to ask, but the word is stuck at the back of my throat. My hands ball to fists at my sides. Ford would *kill* me if he knew I opened that door.

Even if he didn't, the people outside could.

Making a hasty decision, I rush to press the intercom again. "Are either of you sick?"

The officers share a look before the female speaks into the intercom again. "No."

Maybe it doesn't matter anyway, I tell myself as I straighten my back and rush down the hall. *Maybe the gene therapy worked and I'm not even sick anymore.*

It's what I'd been telling Ford for years. I *begged* him to take me to get re-tested at a *real* hospital. With *real* doctors. But he always refused. *Too much of a risk,* he would say, deep brown eyes hard and lips curling back to reveal shining porcelain veneers. *Don't ask me again, girl.*

There is only one other way I know of to test the theory and it's to go outside. If I die, then Ford is right and it didn't work, but I would've finally found a way to escape him. And if I lived...

I don't see a flaw with either option.

I throw back the deadbolt and twist the lock above the knob. Then I grip the handles of the bar lock and use all my shoulder strength to twist them into the unlocked position, heart hammering in my chest.

With a tug, the door opens without so much as a groan, brushing softly against the rug.

"Paige St. Clare?" The male officer inquires, a brow raised, making me wonder what I must look like. Pale and wide-eyed like some wild thing.

Attempting to school my features, I clear my throat. "Yes."

The male officer removes his hat and folds it into his chest as he bends his head. His kind eyes widen for an instant as they catch mine in the early morning light.

Dutifully, I cast them away like Ford taught me. The reflective silver hue of them unnerves people, and Ford doesn't like people to notice me at all, let alone pay any close attention.

"I'm afraid Mr. Ford won't be coming home," the man says, and I can't help snapping my gaze back up, needing to better understand the implication of his words.

"What?" I snap, all my lessons on proper manners and decorum forgotten.

"Your...*um*," the female officer glances at something on her notepad and then tucks it back into her belt, "adoptive father was in an accident."

The way she says *accident* makes me skeptical, but if she is about to tell me what I think she is, I don't fucking care the reason why.

My eyes go saucer wide. My hope floats. I can barely breathe the words for fear of shattering this beautiful illusion, "Is he dead?"

The officers nod in unison. The female bites her bottom lip and turns, gesturing to where a sleek white police cruiser perches in Ford's otherwise unoccupied driveway. "We're sorry to have to be the ones to tell you this, Miss St. Clare." A pause. A sigh. "But we do need you to come and ID the body."

The body.

Ford's *body.*

Because he is no longer living. Because he is now a dead thing, like the dead things he tortured me with.

Unable to fully grasp the meaning of it all, I find myself nodding, in a sort of daze. *I need to see him dead*, I ration with the part of my mind trying to shy away from the outdoors and from the possibility of illness.

I need to see for myself that his heart isn't beating. Only then will I allow myself to feel the rush of relief trying to balloon beneath the cage of my ribs.

For now, it is merely speculation. A fantasy.

They are Hagrid come to take me to a faraway place where miracles are real. Where villains get their due.

Who am I to say no to that? Consequences be damned.

"All right," I manage. "I'll come with you."

I take a step out the door and the heavy tracker on my ankle chirps, disturbing the silence. I step back, a hot flush clawing up my neck as I lift the hem of my jeans. "Do you know how to take this off?"

The female officer's lips part as she takes in the chunk of black plastic strapped around my limb. The tiny light pulses green, a constant reminder that the thing is armed. That I can't leave.

Beneath the device, bruised and sallow skin catches the cloud-covered sun's gray light. Scars from years of wear shine silver, and more recent sores and shallow cuts streak around the edges of the cuff.

"Oh, honey," the officer reaches out, but draws back when I flinch, her hazel eyes confused and horrified all at once. She kneels down in front of me and gestures to my ankle, drawing a sleek black blade from her belt. "May I?"

It's only plastic; I know she can cut it off. I'd thought of doing the same a million times before, but tampering with it sent an alert to Ford. Tampering with it meant I would be punished.

...but if Ford is dead...

The device clatters to the cement stoop after one easy slice of the officer's blade. The cool morning air stings the sensitive skin around my ankle bone, and I grimace, but the pain is nothing compared to the utter satisfaction gained from listening to the tracker chirp five times and then sputter out, crushed under the boot of the male officer.

I watch, enraptured as the blinking red light wanes until it goes out entirely.

3

"Would you mind coming back to the precinct with us for a few questions?"

The officer gives me an encouraging, albeit strained, grin as she tucks a loose strand of dark-brown hair behind her ear. With one last glance at the shape of Ford beneath the white sheet, I draw the back of my hand over my watery eyes. "Okay," I say and turn away.

I don't get more than half a step. A strange pressure slams down onto my chest. I clutch it, pulse quickening at the foreign sensation.

For an instant, I wonder if I'm having a heart attack and gasp a breath, unable to choke out a plea for help. It's *crushing*. I can't breathe.

Sputtering, I reach out, looking for something to steady me as my head begins to spin, my mind fogged and disconnected without oxygen. I stumble, confused and suffocating until finally, I catch myself.

My hand curls around cold flesh and bone, and I start, my squinted eyes flying open.

A muffled exclamation floats past my ears, but I can't make out the words. The world is fuzzy and unfocused. Everything a blur of white and steel gray under the flickering lights overhead.

Everything except Ford.

He stands in blazing clarity. A myriad of color in a monochrome world. He hunches at the head of the gurney where his deceased body still lies beneath the cloth. His dark eyes stare deep into my soul. His sneer is strong enough to curdle dairy.

A scream lodges in my throat, stoppered by my inability to breathe.

"*Run, girl,*" he says, the words a whisper trailing on a phantom wind. Then louder, more urgent, his face contorting into the blistering red fury that always preceded one of his more zealous punishments. "*Run!*"

The high-pitched peel of a scream burrows into my ears, choked off only when the officer rips my hand from Ford's twitching, putrid flesh. The instant I let go, fingers aching from the force of my grip, the phantom Ford vanishes in a puff of curling black smoke.

Color returns to the room.

Breath returns to my lungs.

The sharp edge of reality chases away the grainy distortion of a moment before. Crystalline lucidity slams back into place, sending me staggering backward.

The only evidence that anything happened at all is the raucous pounding of my pulse thudding wildly in my ears, and the cold, clammy sweat coating my palms and beading over my chest.

The pressure in my lungs fully eases only when the officers drag me from the room. Every step away from Ford granting me another small breath until we make it outside.

I jerk myself away from the officers, and helpless to stop it, I bend with my hands planted firmly on quaking knees and retch onto the street.

"She's in the system," I hear one of the officers whisper just outside the door to the small room where they deposited me. "Looks like she has some mental health issues. Bi-polar. Schizophrenia. Paranoid psychosis. You name it, it's in the file."

"Are you sure?" The female officer who I learned is called Silva asks, and I sense the hesitation in her tone.

"Yeah. Seems our cadaver took the responsibility of watching over her after her mom died in childbirth."

"No family then?"

"None."

A long sigh. "It just doesn't make sense," Officer Silva argues. "She was locked up in that creepy house with a damned tracker on her ankle. She seemed...scared."

The other officer doesn't remark on her comment. There's a rustle of paper and Silva speaks again. "Get me a diviner. I just want to be sure before we hand her over to the state to deal with."

I stop breathing.

Handing me over to the state takes a backseat in the horror-mobile to the mention of a diviner.

They are Nephilim. From what I know, they can see truths and sometimes—if their heritage is enriched with enough angel's blood—events of the past. In the rarest of circumstances, glimpses of the future as well.

One of the news channels covered a story once where the police enlisted the help of a diviner to catch a killer. I wonder if that sort of thing is common practice now.

A ball forms in my throat, and I struggle to swallow it down, not daring to hope.

I strain to hear as the other officer speaks again. "She's nineteen, Silva, a legal adult. If she refuses to—"

"Just get me the damned diviner, Peters."

Peters' heavy footsteps grow faint as he moves away, back toward the subdued swell of conversation and ringing telephones at the entrance to the large building.

I busy myself worrying the hem of my tank top when Silva reenters the small room a moment later, her expression drawn.

She no longer makes an effort to look me in the eyes. It's always the same. At first, they jump to my defense. Pity me. Want to help me. And then when they are presented with Ford's *facts*, their tone changes.

Their defense becomes indifference. Their desire to help dwindles.

But the pity always remains.

It seems even after his death I won't be able escape the lies Ford spun to keep me *safe*. It would almost be funny if it weren't so sad.

"You asked if we were sick," Silva says, edging the words in a way that is neither a statement nor a question, but something in between. Giving me the freedom to decide if I want to respond.

"I have SCID."

Her left brow raises as she folds herself into the brown leather chair on the opposite side of the narrow desk between us.

"My immune system is compromised," I explain. "I get sick a lot easier than healthy people."

I don't bother adding in the fact that if I *do* get sick, I am far more likely to *die* than your average person. This is the longest I've been out of the house in two years. And the furthest I've ever been from the house *ever*.

I don't want to ruin it.

On the way into the precinct an hour before, I could see the glint of sunlight bouncing off the rushing water of the Mississippi river in the distance. Could just make out the curved top of the Gateway Arch across the river in Elisium. Which means The Hinge isn't very far.

From this side, in East St. Louis, it doesn't look like a devil's playground is sprawled over the land of what used to be St. Louis proper. It's hard to imagine that across the metal bridge at The Hinge, Diablim roam freely.

The offspring of humans and demons have many forms, but they all go by that name.

And even though Ford didn't permit me to learn much about them, I know enough from the blare of the television behind his locked bedroom door. I sat and listened there for hours as the news anchors told of the creatures living in the lawless city next door to us. Of the chaos and carnage.

Demonic beasts. Incubi and succubi. Salamanders, necromancers and fallen angels, and who knows what else. They all live there—just a stone's throw away. Some of the Nephilim live there, too, though many have been granted permission to live on our side of the river.

It's a truth universally accepted by everyone except Ford that the offspring of humans and angels can be trusted even though their dark counterparts across the river cannot.

They say the demons can't cross it. That the rushing water acts as a natural sort of deterrent. But some

Diablim *can* cross—if the amount of tainted blood flowing in their veins isn't too great.

Being this close to Elisium makes me shudder with rivaling sensations of revulsion and morbid curiosity. If I'd been allowed, I would have *inhaled* all knowledge of their kind.

Now, I may not ever get the chance. If the police don't send me to a new place to be locked up because of my *'mental instabilities,'* I may still be a dead girl walking.

No doubt one of the hundred people in this building is ill with some sort of ailment my weak immune system will suck up. By tomorrow, I could be hospitalized.

By the end of the week, I could be on a slab next to Ford.

I shiver, trying to suppress the strange image of him hovering over his own corpse at the morgue. A hallucination—it had to be. Yet another side-effect of the pills Ford had me swallow day after day without fail.

They are supposed to boost my immune system, but all they do is leave me feeling heavy-headed and lead-limbed. And sometimes, they make me see things that aren't there. But Ford had been *vivid*.

Not a strange shadow at the edges of my vision, or a foreign voice whispering as I reheat my tea in the microwave.

He was so real I felt as if I could've reached out and touched him.

Hallucination or not, the memory of his twisted face is burned there at the front of my mind, taunting me.

Run, he said. But to where?

Obviously, my subconscious mind is trying to tell me something, and I'm willing to bet it's that I can't trust these people.

The officer in front of me wouldn't hesitate to throw me into an asylum at the first indication that the paperwork now lying face down on her desk holds the truth.

Telling her I saw the ghost of the dead man on the steel table at the morgue would earn me a one-way ticket.

"Paige?" Officer Silva prods, and I realize I missed something she said.

"Hmm?"

"I said that we have your medical records here. I submitted a request for them when we got back to the precinct, along with your adoption paperwork. There's no indication of any sort of autoimmune disease that I can see here."

"I don't understand."

Officer Silva's face pinches, and she pulls her lower lip in between her teeth, inhaling sharply. Her hazel eyes briefly flit to my ankle and the angry red flesh there before returning to my face. "This is a safe space."

Silva folds her fingers together and sets them atop

the desk, watching me carefully. "Is there anything you want to tell me, Paige? About Mr. Ford?"

A tingling numbness works its way into my fingertips, crawling lazily up my arms. I barely heard what came after *there's no record of any autoimmune disease.*

I shake my head and a dull ache forms behind my eyes.

She is wrong.

"I'm sorry, I don't—" I cut myself off, trying to remember what I'd been about to say. A thousand thoughts race and crash through my skull, and I can't piece them together.

It's clearly a mistake. They were missing records or were sent incomplete ones.

"*I don't understand,*" I state more clearly, clenching my hands together in my lap tight enough to bruise. "There's clearly been some mistake."

She taps the spacebar on a keyboard and swivels a square computer monitor to face me. Her slender finger pokes a spot on the screen.

"It says here that you were delivered by a midwife at Mr. Ford's residence. No complications. And here in your immunization record, it says that you were inoculated at two months old, and again at four months old by a private physician."

"No," I interrupt. "No, I was never immunized. Regular immunizations could kill me."

I sigh. They've obviously gotten my record mixed

up with someone else's. I go to say as much, but Silva's grim expression gives me pause.

She turns the screen back to face her, shifting in her seat. "Well, maybe there's something missing here, then," she offers, though I can tell she doesn't believe it herself. "Your medical records cut off abruptly after that. There's no record of any injury or sickness. Have you ever been admitted to a hospital?"

She leans back in her chair, bringing the cap-end of a pen to her lips to gnaw on. Her doubtful tone makes my stomach uneasy again, and I swallow back the taste of bile as it tries to rise in my throat.

"No, Ford always took care of—"

Two sharp raps on the door interrupt me. Silva sits up straighter in her chair, discarding the pen into a drawer in her desk.

"Come in," she calls, straightening her shirt.

The door opens and the other officer from earlier pokes his head in, offering me a small nod and a tight smile before he turns to Silva. "The diviner is here."

4

"So, Paige," the diviner begins, tilting his head at me with patient eyes. "May I call you Paige?"

My mouth is brutally dry, and all my words have crumbled to dust.

He is…*magnificent*.

I can't help gaping. Warring emotions of terror and awe dance through my mind and twitch at my nerve endings. The undeniable urge to *run* makes my knees bounce, but I stay put, transfixed and completely unable to stop staring.

The diviner, something not quite man and not quite angel, is the most beautiful being I've ever beheld in real life or even on screen. He's over six feet tall with broad shoulders and a square jaw. Gently waving auburn hair sweeps low over his left brow, and his eyes…his eyes are like starlight captured beneath a thin pane of glass.

The diviner waits patiently for my response, leaning casually against Silva's desk with his knee bent and corded arms stretched backward to prop him up.

Something about his whole demeanor manages to be relaxed and also poised to spring at the same time. There is no telling his age, either. He could be twenty-five or forty-five, it's anyone's guess. With skin as unlined and unblemished as his, he could even claim he's underage and I might believe him

Finally finding my voice, I croak hoarsely, "Yes. Yes, Paige is fine."

He smiles, and I swear it's all I can do not to drool. Are they all this painfully beautiful? I may have listened to endless news stories about the diviner's kind, the Nephilim, and about the Diablim, too, but I've never seen one.

Not on TV. Not in real life. All I ever had were Ford's description to go by.

Ford gave me access to a massive online library of movies and even had the credit card information saved in the system so I could purchase more. He had subscriptions to most streaming services, too. I watched them from under the comfort of my weighted blankets as the mini projector threw the moving pictures over my one blank wall.

I was allowed fictional movies and books of almost any kind. Ford only censored some documentaries and anything satanic or overly dark in nature.

This man—*this being* is definitely not satanic, and I

don't need a visual reference to see that. He radiates light. Exudes life.

How could Ford have thought the Nephilim to be anything less pure than their angelic forefathers?

How could he describe them as hideous abominations?

"Good," the diviner intones, leaning forward over his knees so we are only inches apart. I hardly remember to what he is referring, but I nod anyway.

"Officer Silva has filled me in a bit on the situation. It seems she believes there are some discrepancies in your file, and that perhaps there's something important you might be hesitant to say."

My breaths come slower at his words, and I grip the edges of the seat I am in to try to calm myself. My eyes dart to the exit, and I squeeze tighter, trying to keep myself rooted in place.

I *hate* rooms with only one exit. It's bad enough that I was deposited in here alone, and it only got worse when I was trapped inside with Silva.

But now I am stuck in this one-exit room with a being who isn't human.

Ford's warnings ring in my ears despite my initial measure of the diviner. I feel like he is good. Like he is safe.

I could be very, *very* wrong.

He's here to help you, I scold myself.

He can save you.

"This isn't an interrogation," the diviner continues.

"You can leave at any time. And if you wish, you can refuse to be read, that is your right."

When I finally meet the diviner's eyes, he recoils at what he sees. The metallic reflective color of my irises unnerves him, too, like it did the other officers. Quickly, I drop my gaze, and the diviner readjusts his position.

"Do I have your permission to begin, Paige?"

Is this really it?

Will the authorities finally believe me? Am I finally going to be free? I could go to the hospital and get tested like I've been begging Ford for the past five years. He had money, lots of it. I wonder if all of it is mine now.

Maybe the house is mine, too, but if it is, I will burn it to the ground. I'll watch gleefully as the wood turns to ash and the metal warps and the glass shatters and melts.

I'll dance around the embers.

"Yes," I manage, and the diviner extends his delicate hands to me.

"Take my hands."

Self-consciously wiping my sweat-slicked palms on the sides of my jeans, I gulp and set them flat against his.

The diviner closes his eyes and inhales deeply as his long fingers close around my hands.

Breathless, I watch his angelic face as he uses his magic to glean information from the skin-on-skin contact. Curiosity piqued, I study our clasped hands, feeling around within myself to see if I can sense his presence in my mind or in my soul or wherever he's rooting around inside me.

He grunts, and I snap my attention back to his face in time to see a scowl form on his lips, growing into something stronger. It savors of disgust.

I'd be disgusted too if I saw what Ford did to me from the outside looking in. Obviously, the diviner had seen enough to know the truth of it all. I can't stand the sick feeling roiling in my gut at his reaction.

I want the serene glow of the diviner's smile to return and wipe out this nagging feeling of dread growing in my belly. I tug my hands, trying to break contact.

The diviner holds tighter, his brows lowering as though he's focusing hard on something.

"*Um*," I murmur, tugging again. "Could you…could you let go, please?"

His fingers press harder, his grip turning painful.

I pull again, another cold sweat blooming over my chest. The hairs on the back of my neck rise.

Beseechingly, I whirl to the door and the blind-covered window, praying to see Silva's shadow outside, but there's nothing. Unbroken light filters between the slats.

"*Let go*," I beg, the chair falling to the floor behind me as I rise too quickly, eyeing the closed door.

I didn't see anyone lock it. If I can just get my hands free…

The diviner releases me suddenly, and I fall back, off-balance, and land hard on my tailbone. My elbow knocks painfully into the upturned chair.

"*Damnit*," I curse, clutching my screeching funny bone.

Tearfully, I meet the diviner's gaze, but the instant our eyes lock, he looks away. All traces of disgust are gone from his face.

"I apologize," he says robotically, moving to right the chair I knocked over but leaving me to lie awkwardly sprawled on the thin carpet. "If you'll just wait here a moment, I'll retrieve Officer Silva."

The door swings open and the door swings shut. The diviner leaves without another word.

Cautiously, so as not to upset my aching backside, I roll to my knees and stand, using the chairback for support.

That was weird.

Why do I get the feeling something isn't right?

Was the diviner simply overcome by everything he saw? It's possible, but then why didn't he *say* something?

Like, I don't know, maybe: *I'm sorry your life has been shit.*

Or: *Don't worry, you're safe now.*

Why don't I feel safer?

Why do I suddenly feel like this is the *least* safe I've ever been?

My disheveled hair brushes over my eyes, and I push it back from my face, smoothing it down.

The bead and leather bracelets on my right wrist rattle as I pace the small section of floor. I twist them round and round, the repetitive motion bringing me back a measure of calm.

"Are you sure?" Silva's voice filters in through the door, and I have to resist the urge to rip it open and beg to be taken home. I want my bed. I want to feel my weighted blankets on my shoulders and let them pool heavily in my lap. My room is my safe place. The *only* safe place.

I don't want to be here anymore.

Ford was right, I shouldn't have left the house.

"Undoubtedly," the diviner replies. "I don't know how he managed to keep her here undetected for so long."

Officer Silva's sigh is so loud I can hear it clearly through the wooden door.

There is an electronic sound and a beep and then Silva speaks again, this time to the backdrop of a staticky radio. "Silva here. We have a 66-17. Ready transport and send back-up to my office."

The pop of a button precedes the sound of steel brushing thick fabric. Silva's shadow outside the window creeps slowly toward the closed door to her office.

"You can go, Remi. Thank you," Silva says tersely, and the diviner's tall shadow chases his soft footfalls away from the office.

I back away from the door, breaths bursting from my lungs.

Running footsteps pound up the hallway outside, and I hear a radio blare to life.

"Transport ready," the garbled voice says over the thudding footfalls.

My back presses hard against the wall as though I can seep into it and hide. A wave of vertigo almost has me falling to my knees, but I remain standing. I've done nothing wrong.

There's been a mistake.

The door bursts open, the hinges straining against the force of a male officer's forceful kick.

A group of faces I don't recognize swarms into the room, filling in all the gaps, closing me in. In the sea of moving bodies and raised weapons, I glimpse Silva's face.

"Officer Silva!" I shout, my voice shrill even to my own ears as I shrink into myself, making my body as small as I can.

I am the girl who chased the white rabbit to Wonderland, eager for adventure, hungry with curiosity, only to be given nonsensical stories and be treated as the villain.

I am a field mouse before a pride of lions.

Perhaps I am dreaming. I don't dare to hope.

"Officer Silva!" I call again, the words choked off by a crackling sob.

Her hazel eyes hold no mercy. There isn't a trace of the woman who sat opposite me in this very office barely an hour before. Her kind, considering gaze is now sharp and uneasy with the strain of regret.

"Get it out of my office," she sneers, leaving me alone with the five other officers in the tight room as she storms out.

A shriek peals from my lungs as the men crowd me and something is pulled over my head. A dark sack blinding me, a cord tightening around my neck.

Rough fingers jerk my hands behind my back, and I fall face-first onto the carpet, blood bursting over my tongue and stars shattering behind my eyelids.

Something hard presses painfully into my back, and I cry out.

"What are you doing? Get off me!"

The words are unintelligible even to my own ears.

The bite of cold metal around my wrists has me trying to jerk my hands free, but they are bound so tightly all it does is cause the thin skin beneath to ache from the hard edge of steel.

I am lifted from the ground and onto my feet, head spinning from the quick, jerky movement. I stumble back, hitting a solid body behind me. A rough hand catches my elbow, the hard press of fingers making the already bruised bone throb.

The pain brings with it a moment of clarity. Reflexively, I throw my head back, rewarded with a hard knock of aching pressure on the back of my skull and the distinct sound of crunching bone and cartilage as a nose breaks.

His hand slides free of my arm and I dart forward, trying to make a beeline for the exit.

A strange crackling sound makes me freeze. I know that sound.

No.

It's my last thought before a white-hot stab of agony tunnels into my back and thirty-thousand volts of electricity send me careening into oblivion.

5

I awake to the smell of stale piss and a man's voice shouting somewhere in the distance. My body aches as if it's been jabbed with a thousand needles—the muscles beneath my clammy skin weak and trembling.

The shouting man draws nearer—or maybe it's me who's drawing nearer to him—his words become discernible through the muffle of the thick black cloth still covering my head.

"Though I walk through the valley of the shadow of death, I will fear no evil: for thou art with me!"

I groan and something shuffles beside me.

Vaguely, I begin to realize I'm in a moving vehicle. Maybe the back of a truck? I can feel the rush of wind over my sun-warmed bare arms, and inside the black bag, it's stifling. Sweat trickles down from my hairline and drops from my chin.

I taste salt and copper.

"For the wicked will be destroyed, but those who trust in the Lord will possess the land!"

All at once, I realize why the shouting man's voice sounds so distant, so muffled. I am hearing it over not only the engine rumbling softly beneath me, but over the sound of rushing water.

The *shhh* and *slap* of waves brushing against a jagged shore can only be one thing. My heart in a vise, I bolt upright and draw in breath to shout, but strong hands muscle me back to my stomach, pressing my head hard against the unyielding metal beneath me. I strain against their hold, but I know it isn't any use. I'm blinded and bound. They are big and I am small. They are stronger.

Like Ford was.

The vehicle passes over a bump and a lancing pain shoots through my abdomen. I curl inward, trying to protect myself from the internal onslaught as the tearing sensation spiderwebs out—my body becoming a conductor of misery.

I have no idea how long it lasts, only that by the time the sensation begins to dissipate, I am panting hard. My insides recoil and twang as if they've been torn out, beaten in a blender and then unceremoniously dumped back inside.

"Any kin in Elisium?" A booming voice ricochets through the atmosphere.

"No," comes the hollered reply from the officer next to me, cut off by the blood-curdling screech of rusted metal hinges and the sweep of chains over pavement.

This isn't happening.

This isn't happening.

Finding my voice around a mouthful of blood, I wriggle against the cuffs and the press of the officer's palm against my head. "Please!" I shout. "You're making a mistake!"

Can't they see that?

I am Paige St. Clare. Immunocompromised-leaves-the-house-once-a-year Paige. *Just* Paige. I am *not* Diablim!

Abruptly, the weight on my back and head vanishes and after a second more, the tight band around my neck eases. Then the black bag is gone, too, leaving me squinting into the blinding furnace of the sun.

A booted foot connects with my hip and I sail over an edge, grasping empty air for something to hold onto before I find the ground beneath me. Just barely breaking my fall with outstretched palms.

Loose dirt and bits of rock drive into the heels of my palms and tear at the knees of my jeans. I flip over and scramble to stand, eyes burning from the light and the saltiness of my sweat and tears. Raising my hands, I inspect the injuries, finding chewed flesh clotted with bits of dirt and shimmering slivers that looked a hell of a lot like glass.

Then, I see what lies beyond the trembling peaks of my fingers. On the bridge, the military-style vehicle I'd been transported in ambles in the opposite direction. The officers watch me from the open back with varying looks of disgust and haughty disdain.

My blood turns cold in my veins as the shining curve of the Gateway Arch glints to my left. On *my* side of the river.

I'm on the wrong side of The Hinge. The police officers in the dust-coated truck retreat back to the mortal side, abandoning me.

This isn't happening.

Mortals don't belong in the Fallen Cities. We don't survive here.

A great iron gate begins to swing closed several meters in front of me, blocking the way back. The crunch of glass behind me sends a violent tremor racing up my spine. I whirl, coming face to face with the largest *thing* I've ever seen.

I was staring at the blackened skin of its calves and now have to crane my neck up and up *and up* to find its face.

A scream withers in my throat. I'm too afraid to make a sound.

Glowing red eyes watch me with cruel interest as a macabre grin splits the creature's face. Its dark, curling horns almost seemed to *ripple* as though on fire.

The demon spreads its mammoth arms wide like a

ringmaster about to announce the greatest show on earth.

In an inhuman voice, he roars, "Welcome to Elisium!"

Two men and a woman appear around the demon's legs. One of the men twirls a length of shining silvery rope in the air like a cowboy's lasso, eyes watching me like a cat would its prey.

Behind me, the metal gates are near to shutting. I can still hear the crank and grind of the hinges.

I pivot and bolt for the gate, finding only a narrow gap remains for escape.

Damn.

Behind me, raucous laughter echoes, and my stomach plummets.

As if I could make it to the gate by sheer force of will alone, I reach out, fingers grasping for the iron.

Please, please, please.

My fingers connect with the eroded metal gates a fraction of a second after they've clanged shut. The sound of a heavy metal bolt sliding home slaughters my last hope of escape.

The rope comes down over me before I can react, and with a vicious tug, it cinches around my waist, forcing my arms down against my rib cage.

The female Diablim appears at my side, wild black eyes searching and a deranged smile on her lips. She draws closer and snakes a hand out, snatching up a section of my hair to drag me closer still. I cry out as she inhales its scent with a strange hooked nose, her black eyes rolling back to reveal red-veined whites.

"*Weak,*" she whispers wetly into my ear. "But no matter, a pretty thing like you will still fetch a handsome price."

6

The Diablim at The Hinge stuff me into the back of a black van.

Into a cage.

My skin burns where it's been rubbed raw in the creases of my elbows with the silver-threaded rope. But that burn isn't nearly as bad as the burn of my mangled palms. Or the sting from where the prods of the stun gun were jabbed into my flesh earlier this morning.

I wince, resettling myself onto the loose bench seat as the van begins to move, the exhaust pipe shuddering before it emits two cacophonous popping sounds.

It smells oddly like cinnamon and hickory in the vehicle. Metal music blares from poor quality speakers up front where the female Diablim and the male who has the lasso sit separated from us in the driver's and passenger's seat.

Warily, I stare unblinking at the other being in the back of the van. It's a young boy. He can't be more than eleven. Maybe twelve. But I know better than to let my guard down based on appearances.

Diablim are known for their trickery. I know from what I gleaned from the seven o'clock news that there are demonic beings—great beasts of old, who can take human form. For all I know, this little boy could be the devil himself.

I draw my knees into my chest and wrap my arms around them before finding my voice again. "Hey!" I shout over the music toward the front. "*Hey!*"

"Keep it down back there!" The male retorts, clanging something that looks like a hooked blade against the metal cage separating us.

"You've made a mistake," I holler. "The police—they messed up. I'm not what they think I—"

"Yeah, yeah," the man waves off my pleas. "We've heard that one before. Your magic might be weak, girl, but it's there."

"I'm human!" I try again, my voice growing shrill. "You *have* to let me go. This is *against the law.*"

My voice breaks on the last words, and I shudder as a hard ball forms in my chest, trying to carry a sob from my lips. I don't let it free. Won't give these bastards the satisfaction of knowing I'm near my breaking point.

I've endured worse, I remind myself.

Much worse.

The male Diablim turns up the volume even higher until I can feel the scattered beats pulsing beneath my feet.

It's no use. They won't listen. I am going to have to get *myself* out of this.

But how? A sour voice asks in the back of my mind.

I've never been to Elisium. I've never even been *outside* without Ford to escort me. And that only happened *at most* once a year on my birthday.

I know nothing of how to survive in a world outside except what I've learned from TV.

If I thought my chances of survival were bad just being with Officer Silva at the precinct, they are slim to none here.

A grimy substance coats the floor of the van, and the air inside is thick and humid. My palms are riddled with all manner of asphalt, dirt, and glass. Some of the cuts are easily half an inch deep.

They will be infected by morning, and I won't survive an infection, not without a hospital. Not without my pills. Definitely not on this side of The Hinge. Do they even *have* hospitals still over here?

There it is. The reality of my situation crushes down on me and a sputtering breath tumbles past my lips in the dark.

I am in Elisium.

In the back of a van with two—no *three*—Diablim. Heading god knows where.

My chest tightens, and I struggle to get air into my lungs, pressing my head between my knees.

Maybe if I go along with their plans…

Maybe if I can get ahold of a weapon…

Maybe…

I jump as the brush of cool fingers strokes over the back of my wrist.

I skitter back, staring into the Diablim's bright blue eyes. A flop of matted brown hair brushes his long lashes. And though his face is covered in streaks of grime, there is no denying his beauty.

The boy shakes his head when I open my mouth to scream, putting a finger to his lips.

He floor, he mouths, revealing two rows of straight white teeth.

Confused, I squint at him. "What?"

The Diablim boy leans in closer, and I hold my breath, terrified he will put some sort of spell on me. Instead, he says just loud enough for me to catch the word over the music. "Healer."

When he pulls away, he's looking at my palms. He gestures to them in silent question.

Hesitant, I press my lips together to stop them quivering and reach my palms out toward him.

If he is a healer, that means he's Nephilim. Half angel.

But he could be lying.

One thing is certain, if I have any hope of escaping this place, I am going to need the use of my hands.

Brows lowering, the boy folds my right hand between his, and I suck in a breath as shooting pains ricochet up my arm. Behind my shuttered eyes, a small burst of amber light flares, and I gasp, tugging my hand away at the raw, burning sensation tingling in my palm.

As I do, tiny bits of glass and dirt fall onto my knees, and as I clutch my hand, the pad of my thumb brushes over smooth skin. Glancing from my hand and back to the boy, I gape incredulously.

Two seconds.

It took him *two seconds* to heal me.

Hope swells in my chest and I spring forward, sitting bold upright. "Can you heal me *inside*?" I ask, almost shouting next to his ear to make sure he can hear me over the blasting music and car horns outside.

He furrows a brow.

"I'm sick," I explain. "I have an autoimmune disease. Can you—"

Before I can finish, the boy presses a hand to my chest. Against the sweat coated flesh just below my neck. I go still.

He closes his eyes.

Please.

Please, please, please.

Ford refused to mingle with angel and demon kind. He *never* would have allowed a Nephilim healer to try healing me. Now Ford is dead. Gone. There's no one to stop me from trying everything I ever wanted to try. Absolutely no one.

I mean, except for the Diablim who have me held prisoner in the back of a van of course.

I'm still sending silent pleas heavenward when the boy removes his hand. He shakes his head.

Not sick, he mouths, dropping his hand. Confused.

He reaches for my other injured hand, and I let him lift it in a daze, but before he can wrap his hands around my palm, the van shudders to stand still.

...not sick?

There's no record of any autoimmune disease, Silva's voice echoes in my skull.

"Not sick," I repeat to myself, as if tasting the words on my tongue can will them to be true. They taste wrong. Sour. Like a lie.

Something pounds on the exterior, and the boy and I scatter apart, flying back to our respective benches. I pull my knees back into my chest, trying to decipher what's happening outside.

I lean forward from my cocoon, peering past the Diablim up front into a sea of slow-moving vehicles and the press of hundreds of bodies. To either side, tented off sections filled with strange wares and even stranger food form rows to hedge in the flow of vehicles and foot traffic.

Horns honk. People holler.

If I look closely, though, it's clear to see they aren't human. Bright red eyes flit this way and that. Between two bodies a tail flicks, the tip of it hooked and barbed. Further in, another *thing* like the one on the bridge stands taller than all the rest of the gathered bodies sweltering under the summer sun.

This one has horns that jut straight out instead of curve upward on either side of its head. It watches over the Diablim in the market space with its thick arms crossed over its massive chest. The demon is guarding something, I realize as we draw near enough to see.

It's an entrance to a low-lying, slightly domed building. The gaping maw of it is pitch black as though it might lead straight into Hell.

"Where are they taking us?" I shout to the boy over the music and the thudding on either side of the van, not caring anymore if the Diablim up front hear me.

The music is turned down so the male Diablim can holler to someone outside the van. "Two!" he shouts and a winged man further inward nods, moving a cement blockade with ease to allow us through.

The Nephilim boy frowns.

"To the demon market," he says, his voice much rougher than a boy his age should sound.

Then he looks away, his shoulders tensing more and more the closer we draw to the black entrance. "To be sold."

7

Turns out the black hole doesn't lead to the *actual* Hell, though it's hard to be sure.

It's as hot as I would think Hell to be. There are Diablim and demons everywhere. And I'm pretty sure I'm one simple cash exchange from being tortured for the rest of my miserable life, so…

Yeah, maybe this is my own personal form of hell.

The Nephilim boy and I are yanked from the van and forced at knifepoint into something I can only describe as a cattle run. The boy first and then me behind him. A barred door is slammed shut behind us.

The jeering crowd around the metal barred channel in the wide-open space crushes against the sides of the bars. Some of them reach inward, trying to touch with clawed fingers. Taunt us. Scare us.

I jump back from one reaching hand only to be

scratched by another behind me. I jerk again when the boy grabs hold of my hand, his blue -eyes as calm as a morning lake.

This boy—*this twelve-year-old boy*—is trying to comfort *me.*

My chest pangs and shame gathers like icy rain to slither down my back. This *boy* is braver than I can ever hope to be.

"Stay in the middle," the boy says, tugging me along. "They won't be able to reach you."

For the first time, I squint ahead of the boy and see where the bulk of the noise is coming from. The cattle run leads us up a ramp and onto an elevated stage. A bright spotlight casts a cold glow over a barely clothed girl shaking at its center.

To the stage's front, a crowd is gathered. Unlike the shouting, jeering creatures on either side of the cattle run, this other crowd is mostly silent save for the occasional call of numbers and a monotone voice speaking so fast I can hardly understand him.

After a moment of silence, as we come to the base of the ramp leading upward onto the stage, the man who's been speaking a million miles a minute calls out, *"Sold!"*

The Diablim girl with the dark hair and red-tinted eyes on stage begins to sob as a man with a barbed tail and tiny horns atop his head steps up onto the stage to claim her.

I tear my hand away from the Nephilim boy and turn to run in the opposite direction.

Hell, no.

The boy grips my hand again, stopping me before I can flee. I try to rip my hand away, but he points harshly to the other end of the run.

There, smiling wickedly through two slats of metal is the female Diablim, a metal rod in her hand. Electricity sparks and dances at its tip.

That's no stun gun.

It's a cattle prod. One of Ford's favorite toys.

There is nowhere to run.

I analyze every corner of the stage as I let the boy pull me up the ramp and into a narrow waiting platform beside another barred door.

He leans back and whispers. "Don't try to run, okay? If you aren't very powerful, they'll kill you for sport."

I read the dual meaning in his words, understanding that I am not worth anything here. I'm not just *not very powerful*. I have *no* power at all. And the second they realize that I'm as good as dead.

The door swings open, and the boy is jerked through, his hand slipping from mine.

My pulse thunders in my ears.

Not fifteen feet away, the boy stands, his small hands fisted at his sides and his face pinched. He does not look afraid. He looks resigned. Accepting.

It makes me sick.

"A healer!" the fast-speaking man announces. "Let's start the bidding at two-thousand, shall we?"

The first number is called and then a second rises to join it, and the auction begins.

Breathless, I grip the bars, watching in horror as the Diablim fight over who gets to own this sweet, *sweet* boy. What will they do with him? How long will he survive?

When the final bid is placed at fifteen-thousand and no one offers another, a hammer is knocked loudly against solid wood.

"Sold!" the auctioneer calls into the mumbling crowd.

The boy is taken a second later. Each of his arms held tightly between two older women with dark hair as they escort him away. He goes without a fight, casting one last look in my direction before he vanishes into the crowd.

Despite the smirking Diablim women jeering over him, he *grins*. I can tell it's meant to encourage me, and my throat burns.

The barred door creaks open, and I'm not ready.

I'm not ready.

I can't do this.

The near uncontrollable urge to run washes over me, but I stifle it, remembering what the boy said.

They'll kill you for sport.

Will they kill me anyway when they figure out I'm not what they think I am?

Is a natural born human worth anything at all in Elisium?

Before I can make a decision one way or the other to attempt to flee, a hot hand curls around my upper arm and throws me forward. I stagger into the spotlight, blinking to try to see through the column of dust-filled light.

My knees want to buckle, but I keep them steady, lifting my chin like the boy did, trying to emulate his bravery.

I may not be able to run yet, but once I am bought—away from this market—maybe then I will get my chance.

I find the safe place in my mind, the one I go to when Ford's punishments get to be so much that I can't stand them. I retreat there, to the numb place, shutting off the fear. Dulling the pain.

One, two, three.

At three, nothing can hurt me.

When I get to three, the walls will be erect, and I will be safe.

It's a coping mechanism I developed when I was about the same age as the boy who was sold before me.

Count to three. At one, let the fear in. Feel it. Accept it.

At two, take a deep breath.

When you get to three, blow out that breath and all the fear and pain with it. Shut it off. It doesn't exist. It's gone. You can't feel it. Not even if you try.

This time, when I opened my eyes, I straighten my spine and watch the crowd, not with terror, but with dull interest.

It's hard to see them through the haze of dusty light, but as my eyes adjust, I can make out their faces well enough. If I am right, there aren't just Diablim in this crowd but Nephilim, too. No angels, though.

Supposedly they were the only ones with the feathery wings portrayed in artworks of old.

"A low-level Diablim, fresh from the other side of The Hinge!" The auctioneer announces in a decidedly *less* excited tone than the one he used to announce the Nephilim boy. "But a pretty one," he adds with the wink of a milky-white eye as he turns to smirk at me. His long, crooked nose twitches with the curl of his thin lips and makes his deep wrinkles strain. He shrugs. "Well, if you can get past the eyes…"

Instinctively, I drop my head and shield my reflective eyes from view.

Whispers fill the space at his words, and I resist the impulse to fall back into the cloying grasp of panic. Stand straighter instead.

"Shall we start the bidding at a thousand?"

"One thousand!" A round-faced Diablim calls, appraising me as though he is doubting my worth of even that paltry amount.

These Diablim can buy a life. Buy a living being for as little as a thousand dollars.

They call the cities where Diablim live the *Fallen Cities* for a reason. Human law doesn't stretch beyond their borders. It's anarchy. Chaos. A place where the strong and wealthy thrive and the poor and weak starve…or apparently, are sold off to the highest bidder.

There are seven of them. Seven cities that've fallen to the Diablim since Lucifer walked the earth for three days and three nights before I was ever born. Only seven in all the world.

I am just the unfortunate soul who happens to live next door to one of them. Why can't Ford have lived in Russia or Japan or even Madagascar? There are no Fallen Cities in those places. None at all.

"Four thousand!" Someone calls out, and I strain to see his face in the dim beyond the column of light. When I do, I wish I hadn't bothered trying.

He is utterly grotesque, with a face half burned, whole chunks of his nose, lips, and cheek charred black or missing entirely. It takes me a second to realize the shimmering ripple in the air surrounding him is from heat. His heat. He hasn't been burned, the Diablim is burning just beneath the surface of the mottled, broken flesh.

A salamander? I am not sure what they look like, but I know they have the ability to wield fire and heat. He could be one of them.

I stiffen when no one counters his offer, pressing my arms hard to my sides to keep them from shaking. Hold my breath. *Please,* I think. *Please not him.*

His black eyes twinkle with the reflection of the spotlight. As menacing as his toothless grin.

Don't give in, Paige, I chastise myself, willing my hands to stop trembling.

I will show them no fear.

I will give them nothing.

If there was anything I learned at the mercy of Ford, it was that once you stopped being afraid, it stopped being fun for them. And when it stopped being fun, they would stop doing it.

The announcer straightens. The drawn-out hiss of the *s* that would end in my being sold to the burning beast leaves his lips. I shut my eyes.

"Fifty thousand."

My heart stops. I peel my eyelids back to find the man who spoke. I search the faces of the crowd but can't find him. Not until movement catches my eye and I watch as a shadowy form cleaves a path through the throng of slavers.

The gathered Diablim fall away, opening a wide channel of bare, dirty cement floor for him to walk unimpeded to the stage.

Voices quiet, replaced by whispers bloomed on devilish lips. A low hum fills my ears and a hush falls over the crowd.

The advancing Diablim stands several inches taller

than most of the humanoid Diablim around him. His long black jacket is blown open in the front to reveal a loose cotton shirt tucked down into the trim, belted waist of his dark denim jeans.

The Diablim's disheveled raven-black hair waves low over his brow, concealing most of his face in shadow. His presence commands attention from the throng.

"Fifty thousand," he repeats to the dumbstruck auctioneer when he finally reaches the front, his voice deep and threatening.

"S-*sold*," the auctioneer croaks. "For fifty thousand."

The Diablim tips his head up to examine his purchase, leveling bright yellow eyes on me. His sharply defined jawline and cheekbones are taut, but otherwise, his expression is emotionless as he watches me quietly for a moment. His piercing stare makes my hair stand on end.

He would seem to be in his late twenties, *if* he were human. Which he most definitely is not.

"Shall I have your purchase delivered, Mr. Kincaid? We can see to it that she's properly bound and won't cause you any problems," the auctioneer nervously asks when the silence stretches on, a wilted grin squirming at the corner of his mouth.

"I think not," the Diablim replies. "She won't be causing any problems. Will you?"

Mr. Kincaid waits for my reply, a dangerous glint in

his eyes and a sharp edge to his words that dares me to disagree.

"No."

His brows lower; disappointment evident in the purse of his full lips. "Pity," he says with a mournful sigh. "Perhaps another time."

❧ 8 ❧

The parted sea of bodies in the demon market buzzes with the hum of animated conversation. Whispered snippets rush past my ears as I put one foot in front of the other, making for the illuminated exit. The Diablim who purchased me on my heels.

"What could he possibly want with a low-level Diablim?" an old crone sneers as I pass.

"Has he ever even bought a slave before?" another inquires in a haughty whisper, though I can't see who.

"Probably overdue for a good fuck," one lanky man with short horns slurs drunkenly to the shorter Diablim at his side. "Think 'bout it—you ever seen him at Midnight Court with a woman? *Pshhh*, I know I ain't!"

Kincaid has to be hearing their lurid speculations; he's only a few steps behind me. But he does nothing, his focus wholly on me. I can feel his gaze as though his unnerving yellow eyes are the same as the press of his long fingers.

The other customers and vendors stare openly, and I'm grateful when the throng of Diablim thins as we exit the squat building.

Sunlight kisses my bare arms with its warmth, and a whip of wind sails up from the river a hundred meters to the right. My pink and purple hair lashes over my face, skewing my view of The Hinge above.

The demon market crouches in its shadow. It's a wonder I didn't notice it from above, but then...I'd been more than a little distracted.

I peer back across the Mississippi, trying to gauge the distance.

If it's true that demons can't cross rivers, then all I would have to do is make it to the bank and throw myself in.

My feet move of their own accord, a slight pivot and a tiny step.

"I wouldn't do that if I were you." Kincaid's rough voice fills my ears, and I jerk back. "You'll never make it across."

In a knee-jerk reflex, I turn to glare at him, earning myself a curious tilt of his brow. "But if you'd like to try your luck," he amends. "I'll give you a three second head start."

When I make no reply, he leans in closer to my side,

putting his mouth level with my ear. "Go on, *Na'vazēm*. Run."

When I don't immediately bolt, the bastard chuckles to himself and jerks his chin toward a parked black town car. The thing is ancient but pristine. It looks like something straight out of The Godfather.

The silhouette of a driver sitting erect in the driver's seat and the low rumble of the engine tell me the vehicle has been waiting for Kincaid's return.

The exit area is a roadway where what look to be poorer classes of Diablim gather cross-legged on the sides of the street to peddle wares from bits of cloth instead of tents and tables.

There are no other cars on the street—in fact, there is a clearly marked sign down the road that says *foot traffic only*. But I get the feeling Kincaid isn't someone who has to play by the rules.

Just my luck.

Kincaid pauses with his hand on the polished silver handle of the back door. "Come," he calls back without bothering to turn. "I have things to do."

"Who are you?" I blurt the question without thinking, fisting my hands and refusing to move.

His head tilts so I can just see the side profile of his face: the glint of golden yellow eyes in the sun, the sharp, angry line of his jaw.

"Precisely what *I* would like to know," he spits back, all the cruel amusement vanishing from his tone. "Who and *what*? Now—get in the car."

My throat constricts.

*But I was finally free...*a tiny voice cries within. *I can't be a prisoner again.*

I can't.

"Get. In. The. Car."

With one last wistful glance toward the river I can't reach, I bow my head and stomp to the car, folding myself into the backseat when Kincaid opens the door.

When Kincaid slides in next to me, his jacket brushing my shoulder, I press myself into the opposite door, getting as far away from him as I can in the cramped space.

Warning bells go off inside like blaring sirens.

I am in the backseat of a town car in *Elisium* with someone who might very well be one of the most powerful demonic beings in the Fallen City—if how he was treated in the market is any indication.

Screwed doesn't even begin to cover what I am right now.

I am totally, epically, royally fucked.

"What are you going to do with me?" I ask as the driver, a man whose face I have yet to see, pulls the car around, narrowly missing two Diablim women. One, I notice, clutched a smoldering babe to her breast. They are both steaming. Their skin charred and lined with rivers of what could be magma. Salamanders. They must be.

I've heard of the deformations some of them

possess from too much watering down of the Diablim bloodline.

I wonder if it hurts. If the human part of them rebels against their Diablim blood. If they live in burning agony every minute of the day.

"I asked you a question," I bite out, tearing my gaze from the burning woman and her child, sounding braver than I feel. But when I chance a look at the Mr. Kincaid's face, he is studying me. His brows drawn and eyes cast in shadow.

"I'll be the one asking the questions."

What can this creature possibly want to know that *I* can tell him?

"What are you?"

My pulse begins to thrum in my ears. *Human*, I want to say. *This is all a mistake. I'm just human.*

But something tells me that wouldn't be wise.

This monster thinks he purchased a low-level Diablim slave. What will he do if he finds out I'm human? Useless? He clearly thinks I'm something more than what the announcer told the crowd back at the market.

"Did he send you to spy on me? Is that it?"

Confused, I fight for something to say, but lamely only come up with, "Who?"

The demon Kincaid turns on me with a furious sneer, his eyes ablaze and teeth bared. "Don't you lie to me, wench."

I cower back against the window, feeling around

behind my back for the handle. We're entering a suburban area with lots of narrow streets and wide yards with high fences. If I can find a place to hide, then maybe...

Kincaid's eyelids lower, his gaze far away as he seems to consider another option. -

"Or was it one of *them*?" he breathes. "One of my brothers? It would be so like them to place you in my path like a gift," he says with a wicked lilt to his voice, face twisting in disgust as he flicks a lock of my multi-colored hair. "Bow and all."

"I-I don't know what you're talking—"

"They would know I wouldn't be able to resist the bait. A pure-blooded Diablim masquerading as a...a common street urchin. Your power *barely* concealed." He laughs darkly, rubbing a palm roughly across his jaw.

I stare close-lipped as he speaks, waiting for him to strike. He has that look about him. The same sheen of madness to his eyes that Ford got when he was about to lose it.

"And you just *happen* to be at the market when I'm passing through."

He shakes his head then turns to me with triumphant disdain. "Where are they then, hmm? What are they playing at?"

My lips part but no words come out.

Is it more dangerous to be a useless human or the thing he thinks I am? By the way he's looking at me now, I have to guess if I were the latter, I wouldn't be long for this world.

"I'm not what you think I am," I manage, and as soon as the words leave my lips, the floodgates were open. "I-I'm just a girl. Human. They brought me across The Hinge this morning. It was some sort of mistake. The diviner said something to the officer and—"

The town car stops, and Kincaid wrenches me from the car so fast and so roughly, my head rattles and spins.

He shoves me *hard* against the car, pins me there. "You *will* tell me the truth," he growls. "Or I'll send you back to the pit you came from. Got it?"

"I'm not lying," I sputter, trying to jerk my arms free from his bruising grip.

His silence is more terrifying than anything he could say.

Without a word, he drags me around the car and toward a massive structure with tall white pillars. I barely register being dragged up a short flight of stairs and through a door the Diablim kicks open before I am tossed onto a hardwood floor.

My hip bone smarts with the impact and my one still-injured palm screams as the tiny shards of glass are driven further into my flesh, making the tiny lacerations bleed anew. I bite off a whimper and lift my head just in time to see a heavy wooden door slam behind me with Kincaid on the other side.

The metallic knock of a lock being driven home might as well have been a gunshot in the dim room.

"I'm not lying!" I scream through the wooden pane, shakily rising to my feet until I am falling against the door. My good hand uselessly tugs at the handle. "Her name was Officer Silva!" I shout at him, emboldened by the separation of the door between us. "I was taken at The Hinge this morning after they dumped me on the other side. Please! Just let me go!"

Kincaid's footfalls grow fainter as he moves away from the door. The old floor creaks and groans beneath his weight until there is only silence.

9

He left me here for two days.

The room is dust-coated and shabby. With no windows and only the door I'd been tossed through for a means of escape. I tried the lock more times than I care to admit once I'd finished picking all the glass and dirt from my palm.

There is a small bathroom, more of a closet, with barely enough space for a person to fit inside with the skinny sink and low toilet. Good thing I'm small. Barely five-five and scrawny from underfeeding.

If Kincaid thinks he can motivate me with starvation, he's in for a surprise. I've gone far longer without food. And lucky me, this room has a working sink.

I can't be certain the water is potable, but when faced with a choice between death by dehydration and a possible stomach bug, the decision is easy.

A person can survive without water for only three days.

But I can go without food for nearly three weeks.

Ford put that to the test once, making me suffer for upwards of eighteen days.

I'd allowed that to happen just that once, and then never again.

The creaky mattress sighs beneath me as I sit, the coiled springs within poking at my backside.

It'd been stripped bare when Kincaid threw me in here. There was nothing in the room save for mice droppings and this mattress. Old and stained, it leaned, the middle sagging against one of the wallpapered walls with a threadbare sheet slung over one side.

The style of the wallpaper, yellowed with age, paired with the thick crown molding at the ceiling makes me guess it's an old estate home. Built in the Victorian, or maybe more of a Greek style.

It reminds me of Austen's descriptions of Netherfield Park.

From the tall columns I glimpsed out front to this wallpaper. Even the worn wood floor, scuffed from years of use without replacement or resurfacing. It all screams Austen even though none of those beautiful places from her books could have ever been owned by a thing like Kincaid.

With nothing but my thoughts to accompany me, I do what I always did when Ford locked me away, falling back into that safe place in my mind.

A place where I am not being held hostage by a monster. Where there is no Elisium and no possibility I've been lied to my entire life about my illness—that last one is a fucking doozy.

If it were just Officer Silva saying it, I could have dismissed it as improper record-keeping.

But the Nephilim boy said it, too.

Not sick, he mouthed in the back of the slave seller's van. I mean, it would explain why I'm not sick yet.

I should be.

In my dark, safe place, I replay the Wizard of Oz in my mind start to finish to keep my mind off it. It's one of many movies I've watched enough times to recite the entire thing word for word.

When that is finished, I recite Poe.

And when I finally whisper the last line of The Raven, I sigh, my eyes growing heavy despite my stomach's attempt to keep me awake with its hollow aching and loud gurgles.

I am nearly asleep, half-delirious, when the door opens and the sound of something scraping over the floor wakes me.

In the soft light illuminating the room from the bathroom in the corner, I see the glint of metal.

The door closes again before I can see if it's Kincaid outside, and I sag in relief against the rusted springs when he doesn't try to come in. I wait, listening to make sure he's gone. Following his footsteps is a strange jingling. Like a tiny bell.

Once both sounds have gone, I relax, sliding from the mattress and lifting my weary head. On hands and knees, trying to see through the dizzy blur to make out what he kicked through the door, I crawl toward it. The skitter of tiny claws on wood tells me what I need to know only a second before the smell reaches me.

Food.

I race the mouse to my meal, frantic as I snatch up the plate from the floor and fall heavily onto my backside, crossing my legs and holding it high out of the rodent's reach.

It squeaks, and I can see its tiny, shining black eyes in the dark.

"Sorry," I croak, breathless. "You'll have to steal crumbs from someone else."

When I'm satisfied the little scavenger has left, I lower the plate to inspect what it carries.

My stomach groans loudly. I can almost hear it shouting at me to eat, but I don't.

Not yet.

Salivating, I study the meager meal of stale-looking bread, a knob of butter, and a scattering of ripe red grapes. I grin.

With trembling fingers, I pull the bread in half, then in half again. I tug the corner of the sheet over from where it lies draped on the edge of my lumpy mattress and set the plate in my lap as I tear the sheet in half diagonally down the middle. It takes more effort than it should. My body is weakened. My fingertips numb.

I tuck three pieces of the bread into the middle, sandwiching a fingerful of butter between two of the chunks. I fold the sheet and drop in a few grapes, folding it again and then twisting it and tugging a bracelet from my wrist to secure the small bounty in a bundle.

My excitement quickly wanes. If left on the floor, or even on the bed, the mice can still get to it.

I consider emptying the tank of the toilet—I've used that trick once before—but it would mean being unable to flush. I can deal with that for a while, but it's messy, smelly business, and I'd rather not.

Spying an old hanging hook protruding from the ceiling in the front corner of the room, I amble to my feet, plate in one hand, makeshift sack in the other.

There's a small cut-in near that corner which may have once held a window seat. I use it to lift myself high enough to loop a corner of the fabric around the hook and tie it off, watching my plate below like a hawk until I'm finished.

Satisfied no mouse can steal from it this high off the ground, I smirk and settle myself into the nook, pulling the walnut sized chunk of bread from the plate for a tiny bite.

✤ 10 ✤

Two more days Kincaid leaves me in the room.

I awake only once more to the sound of scraping and a plate being shoved in. Joke is on him, though. I haven't even finished with my first food hoard before the second comes. He's a pitiful jailor.

I expected more from a Diablim.

It has been a full waking cycle and most of a sleeping cycle when I awaken the day after the last food delivery. It would be impossible to tell if it's day or night for the lack of windows, but…the door is open.

Through it, I can see it's dark. The house beyond the prison of this room is swathed in the eerie bluish hue of moonlight. I still, listening for any hint of sound.

When I hear none, I push myself to my elbows and rub my eyes, blinking away the film of sleep to make sure I'm hallucinating, or still dreaming.

I'm not.

The door stands wide open, and there isn't a sound to be heard through the massive house. Not the creak of a floorboard or even the protests of old plumbing in the walls.

A miasmal silence spurs my pulse to pounding as I force myself up, wiping my clammy hands on the thighs of my jeans. My bracelets clatter together on my wrist, the black beads knocking into the white ones.

Grimacing, I cautiously remove each one, setting them down soundlessly onto the mattress. I can't remember the last time I've taken them off without the intent to put them back on.

Each one marks a time when Ford allowed me to leave the house. Nine of them. Each purchased on my birthday—the one day a year Ford gave me whatever I wanted, save for my permanent freedom.

When I was fourteen, I asked to get my ears pierced. Ford hated that, but it was the one day a year he wouldn't deny me a request.

So, when I was fifteen, I asked to get them pierced again.

It went on like that every year for my birthday.

He would give me a bracelet and then ask me what I wanted. I chose the things that I thought would annoy him the most.

Piercings.

A tattoo.

Pink and purple hair.

If it got me out of the house *and* pissed off Ford, then that was what I asked for.

It was the one day a year there were no repercussions.

Once the bracelets are off, I sigh, feeling like I've dropped fifty pounds from my shoulders instead of one pound from my wrist. Ford expected me to wear those bracelets. He caught me with them off only once and I paid for it. Once he was finished with the hose, he watched me put each one back into place and only left when I had all of them back on.

Ungrateful, he called me.

But he isn't here to tell me to put them back on anymore. He won't ever be here again. The thought gives me strength, even though some small broken part of me deep, *deep* down aches at his loss even though I'm trying hard to ignore it.

Ford was all I'd known for nineteen years…

I turn to the open door and lengthen my spine, curling my fingers into fists at my sides. I won't wait nineteen years for escape to find me this time.

I'm not going to be a prisoner again. Sick or not, I am getting the hell out of here because the truth is, I'd rather die than waste my life locked inside for another minute.

Though, I can't help noticing how much better I feel since the officers came to collect me on Ford's doorstep. Not sick at all, but more alert than I've ever been. And even though I should feel weak from the lack of proper sustenance, I don't—at least, not like I normally would. I feel oddly…healthy.

It has to be one of the weirdest things I've ever felt.

On tiptoe, I creep to my store of food and step up onto the ledge to pull it down from the hook, wrapping the sheet around my fist. I'm acutely aware that the door didn't open itself. That this is likely some sort of trap. Or maybe a test.

Ford tested me in much the same way.

Leaving my bedroom door and the front door unlocked several times to see what I would do—if I would attempt to leave.

I did of course.

Until he made me never want to try again.

I peer out the door, listening with eyes closed and held breath for anything at all. Tentatively, I slide one foot over the threshold, and let the air escape from my lungs when nothing happens.

No alarms trigger.

No scary beastie emerges from the shadows to eat me.

Kincaid is nowhere to be seen.

The room Kincaid is keeping me in is near to a wide staircase placed in the center of an even wider foyer. About thirty steps away to my right is the front door. The large windows above it in the high-ceilinged entry give away that it's nearing dawn.

Though the sky is still filled with the light of the moon and speckle of stars, it's begun to brighten. The deep gray clouds turning shades of eggplant and lavender on their bellies.

Go, Paige, I scold myself, grinding my teeth in frustration at my body's natural response to stay put. *This isn't Ford's house*, I tell myself. Though I can't help but check each corner of the large entryway for cameras. Searching for any hint of an alarm system console near the door. There is nothing like that.

One, two, three.

I step toward the door, conscious of the small slapping sound my bare feet make against the wood. Once past the staircase, I hesitate. The wide opening on the opposite side leads to what looks like a sitting room.

It's vacant, but it isn't the room itself that catches my eye. Beyond that room, through another doorway, there's a light on.

I can just make out the edge of a bookcase. The tomes packed tightly upon its shelves don't possess the colorful, lettered spines of fiction. They are thick-spined and leather-bound. Without any titles at all.

Biting my lower lip, I curse myself, glancing between the shelves and the door only fifteen more steps away. They are magic books. I just know it.

This is the home of a Diablim. A powerful Diablim.

My mind whirs with all the possibilities—all the *knowledge* books like those could possess.

Ford hadn't ever included anything to do with Nephilim or Diablim, or even angels or demons in any of our lessons other than to condition me against them. To attempt to teach me to fear and loathe their kind.

It mostly backfired, making me all the more curious about the one subject I was forbidden to learn about.

If I could just grab even one of those books.

My fingers twitch, and I lick my lips. My feet move of their own accord. One step, then two.

Stop.

No.

I grit my teeth, cursing myself in a whisper beneath my breath. What the hell am I doing?

I spin around, intending to march straight out that door and then *run.* Run and not stop until I find a way back. I'll figure out what to do after that once I'm safely away from this place.

A weight like an anvil drops in my gut and I take in the figure now standing in front of the door like a gate-keeper of Hell.

Kincaid's yellow eyes spark in the murky foyer. They are all I can see save for his tall, broad-shouldered shape. I gasp, my body bracing for punishment, aching to run.

"Good," Kincaid says, his voice a deep and cold monotone. "You're awake."

He steps forward into the light, and I can't help but notice how the moonlight glints on strands of colors close to silver and blue threading his raven-black hair. His jaw is sharpened by shadow and his cheeks paled by moonlight.

His yellow eyes skim the makeshift sack clenched in my fist and his brow furrows. "Come," he says and turns without another word, showing me his back as he walks through the sitting room and into the room with the books.

Briefly, I consider making a run for the door, but think better of it. If the Diablim bastard can sneak by me and get all the way to the front door in a matter of a few seconds without a sound, there is no chance of escape now that he knows I'm awake.

Death by Diablim now or bide my time to escape another day?

Turns out a slow and painful death isn't as attractive as spending a bit longer as a prisoner after all.

In the back of my mind, I pray the Diablim in the demon slave market was wrong about what Kincaid wanted from me. Maybe the reason he hasn't been seen with women around Elisium society is because he prefers the company of men.

Not because none can stand him long enough to bed him.

That was one thing Ford never used against me. He hurt me. Manipulated me. Kept me hidden away. But he never touched me like *that*.

No one had. Not ever.

Dutifully, with a lump in my throat, I follow the shadow of Kincaid into the room with the light.

The shelves of leather-bound tomes stretch on across the far wall, covering it in shades of brown, mahogany, and black buttery leather. It's something like a library. A fireplace with nothing but cold ash and soot squats against the wall opposite the books, a single wingback chair and side table in front of it.

The rest of the space is empty. Like Kincaid neglected to finish unpacking when he moved in. A tinny bell jingles cheerfully, and I squint to see a plume of white fur vanish around the edge of the bookcase, exiting through a door identical to the one I'm standing in.

A cat?

I hope it's a cat and not some hell beast waiting for its chance to take a swipe at Kincaid's new guest.

I worry the hem of my shirt in the doorway as Kincaid moves gracefully to the chair, curling his fingers around the high back of it. "Please," he says bitterly. "*Sit.*"

When I make no move to obey, he cuts his yellow eyes to me and his cheekbones flare. Something in the look he gives me makes my airway seize. I move, stomach fluttering as I cross the room and slowly sink into the deep crimson cushion.

The hairs on the back of my neck prick as he watches me from behind, unmoving.

"What is it you want?" I ask, finding my voice, but not daring to turn around and face him.

I asked him this question once before and he gave me no answer. I hardly expect one from him now, but I can't help asking. I can't help *needing* to know what I'm in for.

His hands slide from the chair back and he slithers into view as he comes around the chair to perch next to the dead fireplace. Kincaid stacks three logs in its ash-coated mouth. When he's finished, a fire sparks to life. I didn't see him draw a match or a lighter.

One second there was no fire, the next the wood had already caught. Without the need for kindling or paper to help it along.

A salamander then?

No. That didn't seem right. Salamanders are low level Diablim. Possessing only power over flame and nothing more.

A salamander wouldn't have evoked that kind of reaction from the crowd back at the demon market.

Kincaid rises, and I ready myself to feel the sting of his striking fist. Or maybe the branding of an iron poker heated in his magically started fire.

But when I squint my eyes open, I find him standing there, staring down at me curiously. His lush lips dip down at one corner, as though he is unimpressed with what he sees.

"You didn't lie," he says.

"You still haven't told me what you want from me," I blurt, emboldened by the fact that he didn't seem intent on harming me, at least not right now.

But as soon as the words leave my lips, I know I'm wrong.

Kincaid's eyes blaze at my haughty tone and his hands strike the winged back of the chair on either side of my head. "I am not to be trifled with. *Do you understand?*"

Pressed as far back into the cushion as I can be, I do nothing but nod. Fascinated and terrified all at once by the creature before me. He wants to hurt me, I can tell, but…he doesn't. I don't know what to make of that.

"Now, we can do this the easy way, or I can make you tell me what I need to know."

A threat. *There*, now we're in familiar territory.

Kincaid smirks wickedly and a strange sensation washes over me. Like fingers tripping over naked flesh. Like warm breath on my neck. A burgeoning heat writhes in my belly, moving lower until my thighs squeeze from the force of it. I gasp, reflexively closing my eyes and bite back a moan.

It helps to keep my eyes tightly shut, but the feeling lingers there, leaving me breathless and aching with need.

It's a kind of torture unlike any I've endured before.

When I open my eyes again, Kincaid is still there, inches from my face, the longer tendrils of his dark hair brushing over my cheek. "So, *Na'vazēm*, the easy way? Or the hard way?"

"Wh-what do you want to know?"

"Good girl."

Kincaid pulls back, releasing the chair and me from his strange hold. What remains of the sensations leeches away until I'm left feeling oddly drained and cold.

"Are you an incubus?" I ask, my hands shaking as I tightly grip the moth-eaten sheet still wrapped around my fist.

He looks at me as though I've asked him something deeply offensive, and I wish I just kept my damned mouth shut. At least half the times Ford punished me, it was because of things that came out of my mouth. Things I couldn't seem to keep in.

I could behave. I learned to behave.

But my mouth has a way of betraying even my best intentions.

"No," Kincaid replies with a lick of distaste and then washes his hand over his jaw. It's clear he isn't going to elaborate. I'm surprised at my disappointment.

"Tell me about yourself, *Na'vazēm.*"

"It's Paige," I correct, wanting to ask him what exactly *naw-vaw-zeem* means and if it's a demonic language, but I'm not interested in provoking his wrath a second time.

"Tell me about yourself, *Paige*," he corrects, spitting my name as though it tastes foul on his tongue. "It seems you were brought across The Hinge four days ago. The transport was arranged, as you said, by an *Officer Silva* after a diviner determined you were not human. You were deported to Elisium and captured by slavers. Then you were sold at the demon market —to me."

That about sums it up. I have no idea how he was able to find all of that out, but I'm not about to ask.

"It was all a mistake," I begin when it's clear he's waiting for me to explain. It's strange how the words don't ring with as much truth as they did the first time I spoke.

There's been a mistake...

Has there?

I am beginning to doubt.

"The police, they came to my house. My...*Ford* was found dead in the Mississippi. They said they needed me to ID his body."

Everything that happened leading up to my purchase at the slave market tumbled out of me. Kincaid didn't interrupt. He didn't ask any questions. He watched me carefully, as though searching for any hint I may be lying. His eyes darken as I go on, his face pinching.

"And then I was sold to you," I finish, sighing. Feeling like some enormous weight has been lifted from my shoulders only for another new one to take its place.

I know better than to hope Kincaid will let me go, but the unburdening of the information is strangely liberating, even if it won't help.

"The diviner was right," Kincaid says after a slight pause. "You aren't human."

"But—"

"You aren't," he repeats, more forcefully this time.

"Over the past four days, I've felt your power grow. You're no more a human than I am a lamb, *Na'vazēm*. It's why I bought you. It's why I thought you were sent here to spy on me."

"Sent by who?"

His brows lower and I bite my tongue, cursing my inability to shut up.

Ignoring my question, Kincaid draws in a breath. "You said you're ill?"

I drop my gaze. That is yet another part I'm not certain of anymore, but I answer him anyway. "Yes. I can count on two hands the number of times I've gone beyond my backyard. It's called severe combined immuno—,"

"You do not have this."

"I do. I take pills every day for it. Ford kept me locked up because—"

"Pills?" Kincaid questions, something sparking in his eyes. "What kind of pills? What did they look like?"

"Purple," I reply, confused at his change in demeanor. I show him the size with my fingers. "About this big with a little triangle stamped on one side."

His cat-like eyes widen infinitesimally. "I see."

"What do you—"

"I'll make you a deal," Kincaid interrupts. "If you'll give me forty days, then I will see to it that you are returned to The Hinge."

My breath catches. "Forty days for what?"

"To learn what you are."

"Why?" I ask, careful to keep my voice plaintive and docile even though I want to scream at him that I will *not* remain captive for forty fucking days. Not without a fight.

"Why does it matter? I'm not what you thought. I'm not a spy. Why can't you just let me leave?"

"Because you are an anomaly, *Na'vazēm,* and something tells me you may be a very useful one."

11

I agreed.

What else could I have done?

With my Diablim captor leering over me, an expectant gleam in his cat-like eyes, it would have been impossible to refuse.

"Through there." Kincaid jerks his chin toward the room he's led me to on the second level of the massive house. "Get cleaned up. I'll be back shortly. I have an errand to run."

An...errand?

I school my features into obedience and force a demure nod, dutifully entering the room. It's a bedroom. Or at least, from the shapes covered in thin white sheets, I think it is. A bed is pressed up against the left wall with what looks to be a nightstand next to it. A shape like a vanity stands tall on the wall across from me, next to a square window.

ELENA LAWSON

The darkened shape of a doorway is to my right. I assume it leads to the bathroom where Kincaid wants me to get cleaned up.

"You'll be staying in this room from now on," he adds gruffly, and I turn just enough to catch the tightening of his jaw from the corner of my eye. "Give no grief, *Na'vazēm,* and you will get none. Understand?"

Heart thumping wildly, I nod.

A second later the door shuts behind me and the metallic sound of a key scraping a lock into place makes me shudder.

Kincaid's heavy footfalls fade down the hall, and I make a point of doing exactly as he asked. I go into the bathroom, flinching as I flick on the light, and a row of big round bulbs flare to life above an oval mirror.

I frown as I take in the shower, a vise clamping around my lungs. I don't *do* showers.

Haven't been able to stand one without panicking since I was eight.

But I don't have to worry about how I'm going to wash myself. I don't intend to stick around to use the wax-paper wrapped soaps in the dish by the sink.

Kincaid only needs to think I'm doing as he asked.

I reach into the shower and crank the faucet on to full blast, jerking my hand out before any of the water can hit my arm. The sound alone is enough to make my chest constrict and my blood go cold in my veins.

On hands and knees, I crawl inch-by-inch to the window near the sheet-covered vanity in the bedroom,

86

parking myself below it. Silently, I unwrap what remains of my rationed food and nibble small bites from the bread and pruney bits of fruit that have started to dry into something halfway between a grape and a raisin.

While I eat, I listen, straining to hear past the rushing of water in the adjacent room. It takes a count of two-hundred and fifty-four, but I hear the dull *thud* of a door closing downstairs. Can almost feel the vibration of it through the ancient floorboards.

I count a further ten seconds before rising on wooden knees to peer out the corner of the window.

Headlights wash over the house, blazing into my retinas, and I jerk back, holding my breath until they pass before looking again.

The red taillights of Kincaid's old mobster town car dim as they move further away, down the straight and narrow road opposite the house.

Once I'm certain he won't be able to turn around and see me, demon eyes or not, I stand to survey what I can see from the window.

There are other houses less grand than this one up the street and next door. Further away, in the direction Kincaid went, there are apartment buildings, too. Though not a single house or building as far as I can see has a light on inside. This has to be an abandoned part of the city.

Or maybe it isn't like this by chance but by design.

Maybe Kincaid doesn't like the idea of having neighbors.

All the better for me. It will make my escape that much easier.

I can't believe the bastard actually left.

Wiping the crumbs from my fingertips, I work the ancient window latch until the rust gives way and it creaks backward, allowing me to push it open. It cranks loudly, and I bite down on my tongue so hard I taste the bitter tang of blood.

Below is the roof of the front porch. A steep drop of maybe eight feet will get me down to it. A further ten feet will get me to the ground. It's a distance with the ability to cause minor injury even if I'm careful, major if I am not.

Good thing I'm always careful.

By hanging myself from the ledge, I am able to eat up nearly six of the eight feet and drop the last two, falling into a crouch to keep my slight frame hidden from view.

The night is buzzing with ambient sound.

Cicadas and grasshoppers.

Wind through leafy branches, and distantly, the rush of the river.

I still have no idea how I'm going to get myself out of Elisium. I can't very well wander back across The Hinge. With my own eyes, I saw the great iron gate. I saw the Diablim patrol on one side and had no doubt there would be an even larger human force guarding the mortal side.

The Hinge isn't an option. Which leaves me with few others.

All the other bridges used to cross the river in what was once St. Louis have been destroyed, save for The Hinge. They stop dead where the water begins. Jagged edges dangling over the rushing current from where they've been torn down.

I am not a strong swimmer, so attempting to get across that way is nixed pretty quick. The only other way out is to go around.

The edges of the Fallen City of Elisium are abandoned by humans for fifty miles in any direction not protected by the barrier of running water. At the edge of those fifty miles is a barrier. A low crawling wall all the way around. It's a mere two feet high off the ground.

How does it keep Diablim in, you ask?

Salt.

And runes.

The short walls are constructed with great chunks of black salt mixed right in with the fine concrete. On the outside, special protective runes have been carved. The combination, according to Lacey Lewis of Fox News, is like a one-two punch that demons and their offspring can't even get *near*, let alone cross over.

So, every bridge within the confines of the salted and runed barricade have been torn down. Between the river and the wall—no Diablim can leave unless they go over the bridge at The Hinge.

Except *I* am not Diablim.

...or at least, that's what I have to believe because the alternative is too terrifying—*too fucked up*—to believe. How could a person go so many years without knowing they're part demon?

It just couldn't happen.

If I have any hope of getting home, I have a *long* road ahead of me. I just pray once I get out of Elisium, there won't be too many roadblocks or patrols near the wall.

I can raid abandoned houses outside the city for shoes and clothes and food. I can use them for shelter when I need to rest. I can do this.

I may have spent the bulk of my existence indoors, but that doesn't mean I don't know, at least in theory, how to survive outdoors. Famous films and novels have taught me what life experience couldn't.

I've been secretly preparing for this day for as long as I can remember. Gathering knowledge. Storing it away.

Though I never thought I'd be using it to escape the clutches of a Diablim in Elisium. I thought I'd be escaping Ford. Running away to a new city, or into the woods for a new life, no matter how short because of my illness.

An illness that might not even be real.

The second drop sends daggers of pain shooting up from my heels as I land.

"*Damn*," I curse, rolling my ankles in gentle circles to check that nothing is sprained.

A rustling sound somewhere along the side of the house pushes me into a heedless sprint. I launch myself over the long yard and across the street, tucking myself in behind a neighboring house's hedge to watch breathlessly for a pursuer.

What if Kincaid has groundsmen?

Or bodyguards?

What if his driver lives in the house?

My breaths and pulse only slow after several full minutes of silence with no one approaching.

The evening air chills the clammy sweat on my chest and the back of my neck, making me shiver as I try to get my bearings.

I know I need to go south only because of what I've learned from Lacey Lewis. The distance to a crossable section of river is shorter that way, but there are also more patrols.

Were all river crossings around the walls containing Fallen Cities also manned? Would I be screened before being allowed entry?

Fucking hell.

I have no idea what I'm in for.

The small part of me I cling to that still wants to believe this is all a mistake and I *am* human says there's nothing to worry about. They can't screen what isn't there.

Except, clearly it is.

The diviner at the precinct sensed it. So did the Diablim who captured me at The Hinge. And Kincaid.

I resist the burning urge to cry and stretch to my full height, scanning the darkened, midnight street.

The river burbles and hisses to my left.

Examining the sky, I find what I think is the north star at my back.

"Okay then," I whisper to the night. "This way it is."

12

I am not Paige St. Clare.

Not a feeble and inexperienced nineteen-year-old with enough issues to drive even the most level-headed person to the brink of insanity.

I am Katniss.

I am Lara Croft.

I am the Black Widow.

I am the strong heroine of a story not yet written.

A shriek blooms from my chest, stopped dead against the dam of my lips. The sound is muffled as I regain composure after the reaching branch of an old willow tree trails a ghostly finger down my arm.

Rushing to conceal myself behind a bus stop trash can, I catch my breath, pressing a hand to my chest.

The streets in this part of the city are all but pitch dark. The streetlamps that were illuminated near Kincaid's mansion are all snuffed out here. Some burned out and others shattered. I have to step around puddles of broken glass on the street as I go to keep from cutting my bare feet.

I keep thinking I can see shadows and the shapes of people at the edges of my vision, but each time I whirl, there's no one there. The wind sounds like whispers threading through my hair, and I'm almost certain if I listened hard enough, I could make out actual words.

So, I don't listen hard. I don't need to be hearing voices on top of everything else right now. Pretending something isn't there when it is is a poor defense mechanism, but a defense mechanism, nonetheless.

For the most part, it seems this area of the city is without power. Or at least, that's what I think for several more blocks until I begin to notice signs of life again.

A light on in an old brownstone apartment building down to the right.

The low hum of distant music thumping indoors somewhere.

Voices down an alley where the flickering orange glow of fire casts long shadows on the brick wall opposite. It pops and crackles to the tune of inhuman laughter.

I almost turn around. Almost go back.

Instead, I grit my teeth and carry on, sprinting from trashcan to tree to abandoned car, keeping low. Keeping out of sight.

Once I clear myself from view of the inhabited

alley, I turn down a quieter looking street, finding a flat expanse of land. A park. The raw pads of my feet leave the cracked pavement in favor of overgrown grass. A sign further up reads *Cherokee Park*.

Behind it crouches a graffitied building barely larger than the size of a bus. A public restroom, I decide, peering around it to the rickety old park.

Rusted monkey bars and swings hanging from busted chains.

This park hasn't seen the touch of a child's hand in years. Maybe not at all since the city fell.

I'm liking the look of the blackened buildings nearer to the river than the lit ones along the path I'm currently following. It can't be more than a hundred meters to the other side of the field. I ration that it might be wiser to skirt the edges of the river than to walk down the streets of Elisium hoping not to be spotted.

Of course, there is the risk of falling in, but I trust my footing a hell of a lot more than I trust the streets to remain quiet and vacant through the entire night.

Besides, if Diablim can't cross the river, they have virtually no reason to go anywhere near it. Maybe even being near it is uncomfortable for them. Maybe that's why all the buildings along the river's edge look to be vacant.

It takes me a solid minute to catch my breath before I'm ready. My body isn't used to this form of exertion, and my muscles are already straining.

Strange, though, how I can't think of a time when I've felt better.

My mind is the clearest it's ever been. My thoughts are sharp and focused. My body may be weakened from near-constant dehydration and lack of exercise, but I feel stronger than I did before.

Like if I had to, I could run all night.

Distantly, my mind draws a connection between that newfound strength and freedom of mind with the fact that I haven't taken my pills in several days now. But I'm not ready to analyze that just yet.

Breath caught, I count to three slowly in my head, beginning to bounce on the balls of my feet. I clutch the corner of the weathered building, preparing to use it as a springboard to launch me fasted through the barren field.

One.

Two…*deep breath.*

Three!

I run.

Cool wind whips past my inflamed cheeks. My feet pound dully against the earth and long reeds of grass batter against my legs. The sounds are nothing compared to the flutter of my own heartbeat in my ears, like a trapped bird trying and failing to take flight.

A shadow crosses the face of the moon, and I almost stumble, craning my neck upward. A sound like damp blankets on a line, billowing and snapping in the wind, reverberates in my ears.

I search the field in quick, jerking twists of my head, but find myself alone.

Just another twenty meters. *Run, Paige.*

Don't look back.

But *back* isn't what I need to be wary of. The shadow passes over the moon a second time, and I find the source.

Spiraling ever lower from the clouds above, a great winged beast descends. When it notices I've spotted it, it opens its black maw to reveal fanged teeth in a hissing screech.

The monster's hairless and noseless face stretches long as it opens its mouth impossibly wide—making its black eyes glimmer in the moonlight.

This time, when the scream blooms in my chest, I'm powerless to stop it. I parry the creature, trying to roll into the grass, out from the reach of its taloned fingers.

Not far enough. It's formidable and fast. With a beat of its webbed wings, it changes course and is right on top of me. My skin tears where three razor sharp talons curl into the supple flesh between my neck and shoulder.

I cry out, pushing and kicking and shouting as it sinks its talons in deeper, more securely, and I can feel its pull lifting me from the earth.

No, no, no!

This is not how it's supposed to end. I didn't escape one monster to be torn apart by another.

I dig my blunt fingernails into the fleshy part of the

creature's talon, feeling rubbery flesh pull away from bone and nearly gagging at the *smell.*

Like the putrid stench of trash left to rot in the sun.

I fall back when it releases me, my head connecting with something hard hidden in the grass. I scramble backward, dazed, the world tilting up at an odd angle as I move, making me teeter and sway with every inch I gain.

At least ten feet tall, with a hairless naked body of pockmarked red flesh and protruding bones, it *screams* at me. Rage burns red hot in its black eyes. Its forked tongue slithers over cracked lips.

Before I can even think about trying to stand—to run, it lunges forward, wings fanning out behind it.

I know I may as well already be dead, but I raise my hands anyway, bracing for its scythe-like talons to cut and slash.

Instead, a blood-curdling screech rips through the air, and I drop my arms in time to see another beast attacking the red-skinned *thing* that was trying to kill me.

It tears one of the creature's leathery wings from its back as though plucking the wing from a fly. Sharp yellow eyes roll over me as it sneers in my direction, allowing the other demon an opening to strike.

The new demon, whose skin is black as obsidian but matte as ashes, bleeds red as a gash is opened across its bare chest. It roars, bearing down on the red creature with a renewed fervor and begins to tear it limb from limb.

Its silvery horns glint in the light as blood splatters my face and fans over the grass.

It takes me longer than it should, but I am on my feet. I run.

Head still off-kilter and legs sloppy, I make for the river. It's my only hope of escape. The cold pull of its current is a weapon I can wield in my defense. It may also kill me, but drowning seems a lot less awful than having my arms and legs ripped off, too.

The shrill cries of the dying demon at my back abruptly cut off and the air thickens with a foreboding pressure, clotting the blood in my veins.

I don't hear it coming. Not until it's too late. I clear the last two meters of space between the edge of the field and the cracked pavement road. I whirl, taking in too-familiar yellow eyes before I trip backward over a cement bumper and the lights in my world go out.

❧ 13 ❧

I'm back in the room with the bare mattress and decaying wallpaper when I come to. My eyelids are heavy. My limbs leaden and detached.

Blinking into consciousness, the events that led me here, back to this room, are a blur of half-formed memories. They come crashing into full form only when I move. Blinding pain sizzles in the pocket of tender flesh between my neck and shoulder.

A high-pitched keening sound skirts past my lips as I struggle into a seated position, breathlessly checking to make sure I still have an arm attached at the shoulder.

Not only is it still there, but it's bandaged. Deep red stains form morbid blossoms on the white gauze. Three in a not-quite-perfect row. One for each of the red-skinned creature's talons.

Tenderly, I press two shaking fingers to the injury,

ELENA LAWSON

testing its severity. A sharp sting lances through my shoulder at the feather-light touch.

It's bright in the room. Without any windows and only one dim ceiling light, I know without adjusting myself to look that the door is open. I have no doubt Kincaid is somewhere out there, waiting for me to wake.

Squinting against the brightness, I find I am right. The door *is* open. Through it I can see a slice of the front foyer, bathed in the warm glow of a summer sunrise.

I struggle to piece together my thoughts. Scattered like papers in the wind, I rush to catch them—pin them into place.

It had been Kincaid, I realize. It had to have been him.

He...saved me.

That couldn't be right, though. The Diablim who purchased me wasn't the same creature who tore the winged demon to pieces in the field. That creature had skin so dark it seemed to suck all the light from the universe. It had silvery horns and glowing yellow eyes. It had bulging muscle wrapped thickly around its arms and straining at its broad chest.

And yet...it had been him. In that last moment before I fell, I recognized him in those eyes. The fact that I ended up back *here* in this house, *in this room*, is just confirmation of what I already know.

Kincaid is not an incubus.

He is definitely not a salamander, either.

He's something else.

A thing I've never heard described on the seven o'clock news or in any book I've ever owned.

What are you? I silently ask the void space outside the door, as if it can answer my thoughts, and shudder, fear at my situation gripping me anew.

Okay, Paige, take stock.

Can I stand?

It takes a minute, and my head aches with the motion, but I do. I find that the bracelets I discarded on the mattress before attempting my first escape are digging into the skin of my thighs, and I try rub out the tender markings from the beads. Brush them from the bed and onto the floor where I don't have to look at them.

A thudding pain in the back of my head draws my attention, and I find another injury there. The wiry edge of a stitch pokes my finger, and I go still, tracing the short ridge of puckered flesh at the base of my skull, and the four stitches running up into my hairline. No, wait, into where my hairline *was*. Tiny hairs brush against the pads of my fingers where the hair has been shorn off.

That's not all. I realize that between the stitches and the bandage on my arm, I should be covered in blood. My skin should be itching with dried patches of it. My hair should be matted and stained crimson. My clothes should be…

My clothes.

The black tank top and jeans I'd been wearing for days on end are gone. I'm in nothing but my plain black bra and ratty old panties. The ones with the small hole in a very unfortunate location.

Well, shit.

I lift the wisp-thin half sheet from the mattress and wrap it around me, pulling the corners up to tie behind my neck. Making something like a toga. My injury screams when I lift my arm, but I ignore the pain as best I can.

No way in hell am I going out there half naked. My physical injuries will heal quickly—they always do. But I doubt I'll recover at all if I have to face Kincaid in my holey panties.

Never mind that he clearly already saw me in them.

While inspecting my sheet-toga for gaps of exposed skin, I notice a sheen of silver around my ankle. When I stoop to inspect it, I find a few thin silvery scars criss-crossing my ankle where Ford's tracking device used to rest. Other than that, there's no evidence that I've ever worn it. The shallow cuts have vanished. The bruises have healed.

I shake my head, rationing to myself that perhaps I've been passed out longer than I think.

Not wanting to be snuck up on a second time, I wet my mouth and step tentatively to the door. "Kincaid?" I call into the pitch dark. "Are you out there?"

A jingling sound, like a small bell, grows louder as something nears.

"Kincaid?" I call again, unsure I want to see what sort of critter the Diablim keeps as a pet.

I trip backward as a cat saunters into my doorway and plops down onto its rear. Tiny white paws primly placed at its front. Fluffy white tail flicking this way and that as it watches me with pretty green eyes.

"Oh," I say aloud, unclenching and then lowering myself to a knee with a hand extended. "You aren't so scary."

I wonder at the fact that the big bad Kincaid keeps a fluffy white kitty as a pet, and almost change my mind about touching it. It could be a shapeshifter—like Kincaid. But before I can recoil far enough, the little cat has cleared the distance between us and rubs its cheek against my fingers, back arching and tail erect.

"What's your name?" I ask, brushing my hand over its silky fur as it begins to purr.

Talk about melt your heart.

I've never petted a cat before. Never even seen a live one in person.

Ford brought a few into the dead room over the last few years, along with the corpses of squirrels, mice, and even a dog once.

My stomach turns.

I scratch the creature under its chin and its wet little nose brushes my knuckles. The little silver bell on its thin black collar chimes. Despite myself, I find I'm smiling. I move to give it a little scratch on the top of its head and my hand stiffens.

At first, I think it's injured. Something hard is hidden beneath its long fur. I lean in to get a look, pushing its fur out of the way, and find a small black protrusion.

There's an identical one on the other side of its skull, too.

I draw my hand back, mouth cotton-dry.

The demon cat with its little black horns cranes its neck up at me, bright green eyes demanding attention. It meows, still purring, and rushes forward to rub itself over my shins.

A fucking demonic cat.

Of course, Kincaid has a demonic cat.

Of course, that's a thing.

Why wouldn't it be?

I do my best to step away from the horned kitty, padding to the door with it on my heels as I pray it doesn't decide to attack,

I can take a cat, right?

Yeah. I totally can. Even one-armed.

I nudge the thing away with my toe and whisper, "*Go away.*"

"In here, *Na'vazēm,*" Kincaid's deep baritone carries through the foyer, and I start, accidentally stepping on the cat's tail.

It screeches like the damned and high tails it across the foyer and into the sitting room opposite, pausing only for a second once it's far enough away to hiss violently at me.

Great, now I've pissed off the demonic housecat. Just lovely.

Holding my arm against my chest to try to reduce the amount of movement in my shoulder, I follow the sound of Kincaid's footsteps to the room with the books, allowing myself only a single wistful glance at the front door.

I am not so stupid to try to run again. Not now. Not injured and barely clothed.

When I enter the library-like space, I find Kincaid in the high-backed red chair in front of the fireplace. The hearth is cold with black ash. But the room still feels warm from the heat outside and the company of books.

He sits with legs splayed—the white cat on his lap. His hand rests in its fur, but does not stroke. The cat hisses plaintively at me once more before launching itself from the chair and out of the room.

"I see you've made a friend," Kincaid sneers sarcastically, eyeing me up and down. His piercing yellow stare alights on the bits of bare flesh he can see between swaths of sheer white sheet.

"I-It's not a normal cat," I say awkwardly. "It has horns."

His gaze narrows. "A very astute observation."

I bounce from foot to foot in the entry, unsure

where to look. What to say. The air between us stagnates as he stares unflinchingly, without speaking.

Thanks for saving me but I kind of wish that thing had killed you doesn't seem like the sort of thing I should voice aloud. Instead, I settle on the simplest option.

"You…" I start, but trail off, unsure exactly how to begin. "You saved me."

I edge the words in a question, leaving him the option to confirm or deny.

He doesn't deny it.

"Why?"

"You were expensive," he replies with a hard bite to the words. "Letting you perish would be a waste."

Kincaid leans forward, perching his elbows on his knees. I think I see him wince with the motion, but the expression is gone too quickly to be sure.

He looks up at me from beneath dark lashes, his raven-black hair falling over one brow.

Once again, I am taken aback by his beauty.

Something so evil shouldn't be allowed to be so pretty…

My mind filters back through nature documentaries and my collection of encyclopedias. I remember that sometimes the most beautiful creatures are the most deadly.

The poison dart frog, with its shining blue and black speckled skin. The box jellyfish, with its soft rose color and reflective tentacles. The Peruvian dragon snake, with scales the color of fire and eyes like Sauron's.

That's all Kincaid is. Latently beautiful. Until he's ready to strike.

"Give no grief and you will get none," he says, repeating the warning he gave before he left the house last night—or however long ago that was—I have no idea how long I've been out.

"We had a deal, *Na'vazēm.* And you broke your end."

"How about a do-over?" I offer, wishing I could stuff the words back in.

After that *thing* attacked me in the field…

Now that I've seen with my own eyes, streets and apartments alive with the chatter of Diablim in the night…

I know I'll never make it fifty miles to the nearest river crossing. Not without Kincaid's help. I want to curse myself for even trying, but how could I *not* try.

"A what?" Kincaid asks.

"A do-over," I repeat. "A new bargain."

He squints at me—taking my measure.

"And *why* would I agree to that?"

I gulp. "Because. I didn't barter last time. I would have agreed to whatever you said if I thought there was some way I would be able to escape. I don't think you can blame me for that."

I remember how he'd been disappointed when I told him I would give him no trouble back at the demon market. Well, I'd given him some trouble now. He should be pleased.

"I've never been to Elisium," I continue when he steeples his fingers and presses the tips to his lips, thinking. "I didn't know what I was up against out there."

I force myself to say the next part.

"I didn't know I was safer here…with you."

It isn't completely true, but it isn't a lie either. It's meant to placate him. Stroke his ego. Tell him in so many words that he was right and I should have listened.

It's these little manipulations that I've used to my advantage in the past—to save myself some grief.

If there's anything a psychotic sociopath likes best, it's being told he's right. And you're wrong.

"Don't do that," Kincaid says, his gaze darkening. His sharp cheekbones flare. "Don't stoop to that level. You're better than that."

What?

Kincaid sighs heavily and then purses his lips. After a pause, he drops his hands and raises his eyes back to mine. "Very well. I'm not in the habit of bargaining with my property, but I'll humor you, *Na'vazēm*. Let us see if a new *proper* bargain can be struck. What is it you want?"

What do *I want?*

"Um…"

"Have you not already decided?"

"I—I didn't expect you to agree," I stammer, saying the first thing that comes to mind—the truth.

He lifts a thick brow.

"Very well, allow me to remind you where we left off," he begins, a note of annoyance in his tone. "I require that you remain here, under my care for forty days. I require that you obey *all* of my requests during that time. You will be honest when asked questions. You will cooperate. You will not attempt to leave again."

My blood turns cold.

I'm remembering just how much I didn't like this bargain the first time. Why I had no intention of keeping my word to it.

"In exchange, I offered to return you to The Hinge once the forty days are spent."

I nod. "Right."

"A fair bargain already, is it not?"

But there are holes in this deal. I know enough of his kind to be wary of possible trickery. I need to be smarter than him. More cunning.

"No," I say, more bravely than I feel. "I don't know what I will be subjected to for those forty days. For all I know you could be planning to run some kind of experiments on me. Cut away parts of my flesh and bone for testing. Or try burning me to see if my skin reacts."

I wait for him to deny that he plans to do any of the

things I've just said, but he doesn't, and my stomach sours.

"A fair point," he says instead, leaning back in the chair to cross his arms over his chest. He cocks his head at me. "Go on."

I move a little further into the room, wandering toward the bookcase to run a finger over the leather spines at my eye level.

"And if you're right about me," I continue, hating that I'm even saying it. "Then I may not be able to cross The Hinge at all."

He nods appreciatively. "It's a wonder you were able to once, though I believe I may know the reason why."

A vivid flash of the searching pain I'd felt as the police carted me over the river in the back of their vehicle returns to me, and I lower my hand from the books, finding my one still-injured palm is almost fully healed now.

Curiosity getting the better of me, I turn to the Diablim man at my back and search his face, wanting to find any clue he may be lying, and failing.

He waits for my requests. For me to fill in my end of this bargain. I rack my brain, trying to make sure all the cracks are filled and I can actually get something out of this horrid arrangement.

If only Ford could see me now…making deals with demons.

I shake my head, laughing darkly to myself.

"So, *Na'vazēm*," Kincaid prods. "What do you want in exchange for my forty days?"

I lick my lips. "I want you to get me across," I tell him. "Not just *to* The Hinge. I want you to see me across it."

I don't even know if he has the power to make that happen, but he won't be able to agree to it if he doesn't.

"Smart *Na'vazēm*," he says, eyes sparking. "Yes. I will get you across The Hinge. Anything else?"

Biting my lower lip, I gesture to the books on the shelves. "I want to read these," I tell him. "And I don't want to be locked inside of a room."

I've been locked inside of too many rooms for too much of my life already. "I want a proper room. And freedom to move about the house when I want to."

Kincaid's lips press into a firm line. "Agreed," he says after a moment and begins to rise.

"And one more thing," I add, a ball forming in my throat.

He waits for my request with barely concealed irritation.

"The boy," I say, swallowing past the lump. "The healer boy who was sold before me at the market. I want you to buy him."

He glares at me. "He's already been sold."

Feeling brazen, I square my shoulders. "Those are my terms."

He lowers his head, eyes searching the carpet while

he thinks over my final request. It's a bold one, and I half expect him to deny it, but I had to try.

Watching that boy be dragged off by those women made me ill. I didn't want to imagine what they were doing to him right now.

He helped me without my asking. He healed me. He made me brave when I felt anything but. It would be ungrateful of me not to at least try to help him in return.

If Kincaid bought him, I could watch over him. I could make sure he was safely returned back across The Hinge with me when Kincaid set me free.

My debt to him would be paid.

"And clothes," I add before he can reply. "Can I have some clothes?"

Kincaid eyes me warily.

"The clothes I can do," he says. "The boy…I make no promises. He may already be dead."

"But you'll try?"

"Yes, *Na'vazēm*, I will try."

Without thinking, I extend my hand. It's what you do when you strike a bargain, isn't it?

But when Kincaid moves in, the tiniest smirk curling up one corner of his lips, I regret my decision. When his hand wraps around mine firmly and shakes, his long fingers brushing against my knuckles, I shiver. His scent, like hickory and musk under a hot sun, reaches my nose.

"We have a deal," he says and then grips my hand

harder, drawing me in closer to whisper harshly against my cheek, "And this time, I expect you to honor it."

"I will."

"If you don't," he replies, releasing his hold on me with a dangerous glint in his cat-like eyes. "I will make you regret it."

14

We sit opposite one another at a long table. Kincaid sipping what looks like wine—or maybe blood—from a goblet, heedless of the fact that it's barely ten in the morning.

He watches me with the intensity of a predator stalking prey, but I am emboldened by our bargain. From what little I know, demons are good at finding loopholes, but they don't break their word once a bargain is struck. Kincaid *must* get me back across The Hinge in forty days, *alive*. There is much he could do to me between now and then and I sort of wish I'd been wise enough to add in that he not be able to harm me… but he can't *kill* me.

There is a comfort in knowing that. A reassurance I've never had before.

I eat slowly. After our bargain was struck, Kincaid led me to this dining room, where a place setting was already made at the table. A bowl of sugared oatmeal and small plate of fruit laid out next to a tall glass of water.

As if he already knew exactly how the morning would play out. I'd be lying if I said I didn't find it a bit unnerving.

I stifle a moan as I pop a quarter of a strawberry in my mouth, savoring the tart sweetness of it. It takes everything in me not to stuff my face with the fruit and oats, but I know from painful experience how well that goes on a starved stomach.

If I have any hope of getting even half of this meal down, I must take my time. And it seems Kincaid is intent on watching me take every bite.

Creep.

Though Kincaid takes second place in the murderous stare contest, his demon cat takes the gold medal. It lies, paw tucked beneath its breast in the windowsill across the room. Its body is still, almost rigid, as it watches me. Its fluffy white tail jerks left and right.

I may have made a deal with Kincaid, but I made no such bargain with his demonic feline, and the way it's looking at me...well, let's just say I'm not sure if I can best the cat anymore. There's something ancient and sentient in its bright green eyes. Something unnerving.

Why did I have to go and step on the damned thing's tail.

I dab at the corner of my lips with a napkin and

lean back, needing a moment to digest before I can eat more.

"Are you satisfied?" Kincaid asks, swirling his goblet.

I purse my lips. "For now. I'd like to try to eat a bit more."

He nods. "Very well. I'd planned to allow you to finish your meal before beginning my questions, but it seems I've made a bargain with the slowest eater in all the world."

I scowl.

"Shoot," I say, sipping my glass of water.

He frowns as though confused.

"That means go ahead and ask," I say with maybe a bit too much glee at his discomfort.

He stands, and for a second, I worry I've insulted him to a point of repercussion, but he merely strides to my side of the table and sits on its edge, staring down at me.

If he reaches out, he'll be able to touch me. To attack me. He doesn't, though. Instead, he dips his hand into the breast pocket of his long jacket and draws out a small plastic bag. It's the size of a quarter, and sealed inside it is a single purple pill.

A triangle stamped on one side.

He sets it down triumphantly next to my plate. I can feel his gaze on me, steady and searching as I lift it, turning the little pill over between my fingers.

Is he giving it to me?

Is this his extra insurance to make sure I don't break my side of the bargain a second time?

Give me one pill per day, just enough to ensure I don't die of illness. Just enough to ensure I'll stay for my dose each day.

It would be brilliant if it weren't for the fact that I'd already come to terms with dying for my freedom.

I open the bag and drop the pill into my palm, inspecting it more closely to be certain he's purchased the correct one. I wonder how he was able to get it.

"Is this the same as the pills you spoke of, for your illness?"

I wet my lips. "Yes."

A knot forms between Kincaid's brows. "I thought it might be."

He holds his hand out for the pill, and confused, I hand it back to him. "Are you not going to let me take it?"

"No," he says harshly, dropping the pill onto the distressed wood of the table and then crushing it to dust with his palm. "You will never take these pills while under my roof. If you know what's good for you, *Na'vazēm*, you won't take them at all."

His jaw tightens.

I part my lips to ask the question burning at the back of my throat—dancing at the tip of my tongue—but then I close my lips again instead. Not sure I want to know the answer to it.

What are the pills for?

As though reading my thoughts, Kincaid says, "They are not what you think they are."

Suddenly, the food I've eaten weighs heavily in my stomach, and I have to press a palm to it to quell the urge to be sick.

"What are they for?"

Kincaid turns his yellow eyes back on me, and in them I see an unfettered fury burning wild and hot. "They're poison," he spits. "Diablim take them to null their abilities. To suppress their demon blood so they may walk among humans undetected. Take enough of them, and apparently you can live undetected on the other side of The Hinge for almost two decades."

I don't ask how he knows my age. I assume he got the information however he got the other info about Silva and what happened to me. Which means he may have somehow gotten access to my file. A burning urge to tell him what he found there isn't true, that I'm not crazy, rises like fire in my gut. I snuff it out though and keep my lips sealed tight. I have nothing to prove to this Diablim.

Let him think I'm certifiably insane.

Maybe he'll keep his distance.

"You're sure?" I ask, still digesting the news that the pills Ford has made me take all my life were not for my illness.

That it's likely true I have no illness at all.

That he probably died by Diablim hands trying to

obtain more of them—though that part at least brings me comfort.

"Yes, *Na'vazēm*. It's true."

Bile rises in my throat and hot, angry tears burn in my eyes. "I'm not sick."

It isn't a question, but Kincaid answers me anyway. "No. You are not. At least, not in the way you were led to believe. The poison surely made you weak. Made you feel ill. But soon, what remains of it in your blood will be gone."

He doesn't say any more, but I can tell he wants to. I can almost hear the words he resists putting out into the world.

Once the poison is out of my bloodstream, there will be nothing to stop whatever part of me is Diablim from coming out.

THE ROOM KINCAID GIVES ME IS THE ONE I SNUCK OUT of two days before. It doesn't escape my notice that a new window has been installed. More modern, without any latches or locks. No way to open it at all.

Joy.

At least there *is* a window. It isn't a luxury I had in my room back home.

No. Not home. It was never home.

I wish I'd been specific in my bargaining for a proper room and had asked for one with a bath instead of a shower, but it's a little late for that.

To make it tolerable, I wad up a swath of my toga sheet and stopper the drain with it. The shower has a small square base and glass walls. The base is large enough that I can fill it with about five inches of water from the showerhead.

So that's what I do. Once the drain is plugged, I twist the handle and step away, waiting for it to be filled with my pulse skittering in my ears and a tight, hollow feeling in my gut. Once it's near to spilling out the door, I reach in quickly and turn it off.

The MacGyvering does the trick. It's hardly pleasant, but at least when I come out smelling of the Diablim's honey-lavender soap, I'm the cleanest I've been in nearly a week.

Thank fuck because honestly? I was starting to itch.

There's only one towel and my toga is in tatters from using it to stopper the drain. With limited options, I wrap myself tightly in the towel and exit the bathroom in search of something else to put on until Kincaid makes good on his promise to get me clothes.

I really hope the fact that I wasn't more specific about what sort of clothes I wanted doesn't backfire. If Kincaid has a thing for trickery, he could get me clown clothes. Or skimpy little bralettes and booty shorts. Thankfully, I don't think he's the sort to do either. But I've been wrong before.

I'm still thinking about all the ways Kincaid might be able to mess with the terms of our bargain when all my thoughts go tumbling from a cliff. I'm readjusting the towel, holding it wide to tuck one side of it more firmly to keep it from sliding down when I come face to face with Kincaid.

He's sitting on the sheet-covered bed, one elbow perched on a knee, his thumb and forefinger stroking his chin. His golden-yellow eyes catch the glint of sunlight streaming in from the window. The light makes his irises look like polished yellow sea-glass. Or warmed honey.

I nearly slip, my wet feet sliding over the old hardwood, but regain my composure, snapping the towel back shut as a scalding blush crawls up my neck and into my cheeks.

"Fuck!" I shout, surprising even myself with the volume of the curse.

"You have an interesting way of taking a shower."

My knuckles whiten with my grip on the towel, and I breathe deeply to lower my blood pressure.

"Humans are such prude creatures. It's a shame you weren't raised properly, among your own kind."

I glare at Kincaid. Trying not to think about the fact that I just full-on flashed him. It's too mortifying.

"You could have knocked," I practically growl. "Or waited outside."

He says nothing, and his gaze never once strays from my face.

Sighing, exasperated, I turn around to fix the towel, tucking the corner deep in between my breasts to make sure it stays put this time. "What do you want, Kincaid?"

"I've come to make good on my promise. We're going to purchase clothing."

I turn, needing to see his expression—to make sure he isn't joking. "*We?*"

His brow lifts. "If you'd rather I select them for you, that can be—"

"No," I rush to say, the word coming out maybe a little too forcibly. "No, that's okay. I'll go."

No way I'm letting him decide what I'm going to wear if I can help it.

"Good," he rises to leave.

"What about the boy?" I call after him before he can step out the door. "The healer?"

He pauses but does not turn.

"I've made the inquiry. Now we must wait."

A start, I suppose. I'm about to ask how long he thinks before he'll get an answer when he vanishes from the room. His rich voice booms from the hallway outside, "Be downstairs in five minutes."

That's when I notice what he set next to him on the bed and grimace. It's my clothes. My jeans and black tank top. The left strap of the tank is torn. The jeans are *covered* in blood, dirt, and grass stains. So much so that it almost looks like some morbid work of abstract art.

Almost.

The smell gives them away as being just as dirty as they look.

I glance between them and the door, briefly considering asking Kincaid if he wouldn't mind my borrowing something of his, but decide against it.

I can't forget that a mere few days ago this Diablim had me starved and locked in a dark room. That he threatened to send me back to the pit I came from.

Don't get comfortable, Paige, I tell myself as I pull on my reeking jeans and top.

It's often that when you think you're the safest is when you are the most in danger. And when you think you are the most in danger, you are the safest...because you have prepared.

Getting back across The Hinge will mean believing I am in danger at all times, even when it may seem like I'm not. It's how I survived this long. It's how I will survive these forty days at the mercy of Kincaid.

❧ 15 ❧

We drive through a foreign landscape. At times, the scene viewed from my rear window is downright post-apocalyptic. Dilapidated and crumbling buildings. Abandoned shopping plazas and coffee shops. Vandalized grocery stores with rusted shopping carts desiccating in their cracked lots. Nature overtaking entire houses.

For a while, that's all there is, but infrequently we also come upon inhabited areas, and my eyes widen in surprise. Some parts of these inhabited areas look a lot like neighborhoods back home. Carefully manicured lawns. Clean streets. Working streetlights at inter-sections.

The only difference is the inhabitants themselves. There are some who look like Diablim. With horns and leathery wings. Some taller than any human could be. But most, in fact, nearly look…human.

Completely and utterly human.

For a moment, I think maybe we're somehow out of Elisium, that Kincaid has brought me to safety. That maybe he's decided I'm not worth the trouble of figuring out after all.

Then I remember. I remember how so *many* Diablim lived among humans already before Lucifer walked the earth nearly a quarter century ago. Before he opened the floodgates of Hell and unleashed his horrors upon the earth.

Before there were less of them. Only the ones who could blend in among humans found a place here. Incubi and succubi. Spirit workers and gargoyles and diviners and healers. They *all* look just like us.

Unless you look more closely, *really* closely, I can see now how no one suspected a thing.

A child chases another child through a toy-laden lawn, laughing as she goes. A mother, hands on hips in a doorway surrounded in rose bushes scolds them from afar.

A knot forms in my belly.

This is not what I expected to find here, and I don't know how to feel about it. It seems almost surreal. Like I'm viewing it through a looking glass.

The inhabited neighborhood passes in only a few minutes and we're back into abandoned streets. The driver, a man who never speaks or so much as tilts his head so I can see his face, pulls around what looks like a park.

Signs say there should be pavilions and tennis courts inside it, but there aren't. As far as I can see across the flat expanse of land is crops and some Diablim tending them.

Whatever used to be here in this park has been leveled to convert the green space into a workable field. I see tall corn stalks and rows and rows of apple trees further away as we turn a corner. Little ruffled balls of green lettuce speckle the space between and a creature with purplish skin and long scythe-like fingernails cuts them from the earth and tosses them into a wheelbarrow. It lifts its pure-white eyes to mine and I recoil, looking away.

It's the first of its kind I've seen, or at least, I think it is.

I haven't seen anything that resembles the red-skinned creature with the black eyes and pockmarked flesh that attacked me.

"Can I ask you something?" I turn slightly in Kincaid's direction, peering up at him in the seat next to me. I'd been doing a bang-up job of ignoring his presence until now, and he seems to have been doing the same. When I speak, it takes him a moment to register the words.

I wonder what he was thinking about.

He grunts in reply.

Okay, then.

"That *thing* that attacked me the other night," I say,

fiddling with a stiff stain of something on the hem of my shirt. "What was it?"

He doesn't answer me right away, and I wonder for a moment if he will at all, then he says. "They are called daeva."

"Daeva?" I press, wanting to try the word out for myself.

The term seems vaguely familiar, but I can't remember why. I try to hear the word in the voice of Lacey Lewis from the seven o'clock news to jog my memory, but nothing comes.

Kincaid lifts his eyes heavenward and sighs before settling more comfortably into his seat. "They are ancient spirits. They walked on this plane before the first man ever set foot on it. They're considered deities by some."

"But not by you?"

"No." He scoffs. "They're mostly animal, but smart and cunning. They live on instinct and feed on anything that draws breath. Some are strong enough to take a corporeal form here in Elisium. Others can only manifest as spirit or shadow."

"Oh."

He quirks a brow.

"Are *you* a…a daeva?"

Kincaid looks at me like I've grown another head. His lips twitch into an almost grin, and I'm struck again at how ridiculously perfect he is. He definitely doesn't look like the daeva that attacked me, but he *was* able to take another form.

His matte black skin and silvery horns made him look every inch the demonic creature he is.

"No, *Na'vazēm.* I am not daeva."

I want to shake him.

"Well," I hiss, frustration getting the better of me. "What *are* you then?"

Kincaid smirks and nudges his head toward the window. "We're here," he says, completely ignoring my question.

I groan audibly and look to see where exactly here is.

Kincaid opens the door and before I can register what he's done, his hand closes around my wrist and drags me out with him. I stumble, but he keeps me steady, jerking my arm to right my footing. I try to pull away, but he holds tighter.

Kincaid leans into my side and whispers against my ear. "You will have ten minutes," he says. "And you are not to tell anyone who you are, or where you've come from. Is that clear?"

Finally, I am able to rip my hand away. I rub my wrist, an odd sensation washing over me like a thousand ants crawling over my skin. I clear my throat and nod.

Kincaid presses his fingertips to my lower back and leads me across a street where Diablim mill about with shopping bags. A group of three Diablim women, at least one of which is a salamander, smoke clove cigarettes at the entrance to the tall building in front of us.

Wafting smoke clouds wash over us as we pass through them and into the foyer, clogging my throat and making my nose wrinkle.

I wipe my burning eyes and blink to find we're in some sort of office building.

"I thought you were taking me to get clothes?"

Kincaid gives my back a more forceful nudge and tucks us both into an elevator. "I did," he retorts. "And I am."

A gaggle of Diablim women step up to the elevator as though to get in with us, and I stiffen. One of them is smoldering.

Kincaid steps slightly in front of me, blocking me from their view. The movement catches their attention, and their conversation is abruptly cut off.

"Oh!" The smoldering one exclaims, throwing an arm out to stop her companions from entering. "Mr. Kincaid," she trills with a little bend of her head. "Sorry, we didn't see you."

She corrals the other three women away from the elevator and the doors shut.

"Seriously," I say, getting out from behind Kincaid. "Who are you?"

The amount of smugness radiating off him makes me want to kick him in his stupid face.

I cross my arms over my chest when he doesn't answer, perfectly aware of how childish the gesture is but not caring. "Fine," I snap. "Don't tell me. I don't want to know anyway."

The door pings open and I follow Kincaid out and directly into a shopping area. A Diablim man in a tailored suit wearing an earpiece and tinted sunglasses *indoors* greets us.

"Mr. Kincaid," the security man states roughly.

"Sam," Kincaid says in reply, moving to step past.

"And this is?" the security man inquires, and I think I can see him appraising me from behind the shade of his sunnies.

Kincaid tugs me along behind him and smiles pleasantly at Sam.

No, not pleasantly. That isn't the right word. It's not so much a smile as it is him baring his teeth. "She's with me, Sam," Kincaid replies pointedly. "Is there a problem?"

Sam straightens. "Not at all, my lord."

Without another word, Kincaid lets me loose and gestures vaguely to the store surrounding us.

It reminds me of the fancy shops from shows like Sex in the City. Saks and Bergdorf's. Barney's. Places where only rich people go to shop. One glance at a price tag on a simple white cropped t-shirt tells me I am not wrong.

It costs three hundred dollars.

Not that I care. It won't be my own money I'm spending. You know, since I don't have any. I grab for the simple black t-shirt behind it and start scanning racks farther away for more things that look like they'll fit.

I grimace as I go, noticing how all the clothes have a certain *style* to them. They are tight and torn. Leather and lace. I try to grab for items less…provocative but finding simple cotton blends amid all the strange fabrics and designs is only going to ensure I leave with barely anything at all. So, I give up.

It strikes me as I gather shirt after shirt, trying to make my way toward an area that looks like it has jeans, that we are the only people in this store. There isn't even a shopkeeper.

Now, I've been in many stores, but I've seen enough of them depicted in movies and books to know that something isn't quite right with that.

"Five minutes," Kincaid warns. "I have another errand to run."

I turn away so he can't see me roll my eyes at him. It's then that I decide to give him a real run for his money. I grab everything that looks even *slightly* like it might fit. Sweaters and jeans. T-shirts and tank tops and shorts. Fistfuls of silk and lace panties from a big pink bin that has a plush satin bow on the side.

Several bras that I'm sure cost more than your average car payment. I can barely carry it all.

A couple pairs of panties tumble down from the heavy mountain of clothes piled between my arms when I turn back to Kincaid and raise a brow.

"Pleased with yourself?" he asks, seemingly bored by my attempt to piss him off.

I frown.

"Time's up, *Na'vazēm.*"

Kincaid snaps his fingers and a person materializes next to us. Just fucking *appears*.

I fall flat on my ass and the pile of clothing scatters to the floor, covering my lap and the carpet in a wide blast radius around me. I bite my lip to keep from whimpering at the bruising ache in my tailbone.

The Diablim that blinked into existence is a short man with a balding head of white hair and small wire-framed round glasses. He could be someone's grandpa. Until he opens his mouth.

Two rows of needle-like teeth flash in the fluorescent overhead light and I gasp, crawling backward.

"Oh, miss, you've dropped your things," the creature exclaims, his tone kind and lilting with an accent something between British and Scottish. "Here, let me get these packed for you."

I scrabble to my feet and somehow end up back beside Kincaid. As if he'll protect me from the creepy old man-thing.

I'm still panting when the needle-toothed Diablim scuttles away with my things in his arms, Kincaid chortling quietly in his wake.

𝕾 16 𝕾

Everything I chose fits in three large bags. Kincaid watches me with an amused glimmer in his demonic eyes as I struggle to heft them all the way back through the building and out to the car.

I never saw him pay for them, and when I finally slide into the backseat next to him after stuffing everything in the trunk, I have to wonder if he needed to at all. If my buying half the store to piss him off didn't even faze him because the shopkeeper wouldn't dare charge the infamous Kincaid.

Seriously, who the fuck is this Diablim?

The not knowing was really starting to get to me.

"Where are we going?" I inquire as the nameless, faceless, way-too-quiet driver chauffeurs us through another section of abandoned city and to an old shopping block.

Little mom-and-pop stores with shuttered and broken windows dot the street on either side. Shrubs and trees that were likely once manicured to perfection now grow wild, their roots cracking the sidewalks.

"To see a friend, *Na'vazēm.*"

"I have a name you know," I snap back at him. "Why do you keep calling me *Na'vazēm?*"

I'm completely butchering the pronunciation, but I don't care. "What does that even mean?"

Kincaid eyes me warily, like he tastes something sour on his tongue. I have the presence of mind to know he could lash out at any second, but I am bolder now.

And if I'm being honest, I don't think he will.

Time will tell if that assumption is as foolish as the rational part of my brain is trying to say it is.

"A name gives a thing power," he mutters. "And gives you power *over* a thing."

Something tickles at the edge of my mind. A series I once watched that got me into a lot of trouble when Ford found out what I was watching. It mentioned something like that.

There was a priest…or something…and he needed to learn the name of the demon possessing this creepy little girl to be able to exorcise it back to Hell.

Was it possible that sort of thing was true?

"Maybe in Hell a name gives a thing power, but last I checked, this is still earth and I'm not some demonic spirit you plan to vanquish."

Kincaid turns his hot stare on me, his yellow eyes drilling through me, all the way down until my belly flips and my toes go cold.

He makes no reply.

Then he turns away to look out the window again, his jaw set.

Well *shit*.

"We're here," he says as the car pulls up to the curb and we both step out. This time Kincaid doesn't grab me. He doesn't curl his fingers around my wrist and hold me close to him.

There's no need.

The street is abandoned in both directions for as far as I can see. It looks like a cut scene from a post-apocalyptic movie. Like when that guy wakes up in the hospital in 28 Days Later and finds a world devoid of life. All that's missing are the zombies.

The shops lining the street are rickety, unkept things with shattered windows and soot choked facades.

At least, all of them are except for this one. Kincaid starts toward it and tugs the door open. A bell jingles as he steps inside.

The sign above the door says *Tori's Oddities*. It's clear it's handmade. A long section of old board with the words graffitied on—the board placed crookedly over the sign that used to be there before.

It's impossible to tell what's inside. The windows have been darkened. At first, I think maybe they've been covered over with black spray paint, but as I grow closer, I can see that they're just heavily tinted.

I peer down the street again and a small strangled sound slips between my lips. Down the block, maybe fifty or so paces away, is a woman. She stands amid overgrown weeds above a crack in the concrete side-walk. Her long brown hair waves in a breeze that I can't feel. And her eyes, the lightest shade of gray, watch me unblinking. She does nothing but stand and stare.

The door sweeps open again, and the jingling bell startles me.

Kincaid glares at me from the entrance, then turns his head to check the street as though he anticipates an attacker or thinks we might've been followed. I follow his gaze, ready to point out the strange woman on the sidewalk, but she's already gone.

A shudder rolls over me.

"Get inside," he grits out, holding the door open for me to pass.

I scoot inside, wanting to get out from under his arm, and it's like I've fallen down the rabbit hole.

Not to a new place or a different plane. I can tell I am still firmly in the Fallen City of Elisium. But it's like Ariel's hidden treasure trove in The Little Mermaid.

Or that crazy old witch's cottage in the woods from that one book with the faeries.

It's *filled* to bursting with so many things it's impossible to focus on just one. A wall covered in varying sizes of hooks sports hundreds of silver chains. All different sizes. Different kinds.

Tabletops overflow with bits of tattered cloth and gemstones and candles with strange markings carved into their sides.

Glass cases stand in awkward places amid towers of books piled onto the floors. Inside them, creepy china dolls are clustered so close together it's a wonder they don't burst through the glass. Their eyes watch me, and as Kincaid brushes past, I swear I see a set of glass pupils flick in his direction.

The whole place smells of mothballs and sulfur.

"Tori?" Kincaid calls into the dim shop. "You here?"

There's a tinkling sound, like glass beads, and I crane my neck to see around the case of dolls to find a woman sauntering through a curtain of multicolored beads.

"Kincaid?"

She steps around the doll case, grins, and takes him in. Her slender hands go to her hips. The shop owner looks pretty normal, but there's an air about her that sets my teeth on edge. Tori is at least a full head taller than I am. With unblemished dark skin and pretty features. Full lips and wide violet eyes. She wears a cropped t-shirt that exposes her midriff and a little leather skirt.

There's a strange ashen quality to her skin. Like the dark umber tone has been bleached of some of its color.

Her face breaks into a sneaking grin, and she cocks her head at Kincaid. "Well, if it isn't my favorite lord of the underworld. It's been a while, handsome."

Kincaid rolls his eyes at her greeting, and I notice how for a brief second his gaze alights on me. Taking in my slack jaw and saucer-wide eyes.

Did she just say *lord of the underworld?*

When I can finally pick my jaw up off the floor, I scootch another couple feet away from Kincaid, which seems to please him, which in turn only sets me *more* on edge.

"And your friend?" Tori inquires, her violet-hued gaze flicking in my direction. She takes in my blood-stained and tattered jeans and torn top and her brows pull in. Her cheeky smile vanishes.

"What the hell did you do to her, Kincaid?"

She rushes over to me, inspecting the blood stains covering the neckline of my shirt and the bandage over my shoulder. Sniffs.

"A daeva?"

I recoil from her reaching hand.

Kincaid nods.

Tori purses her lips. "You poor thing."

When she catches sight of my eyes, it's her turn to back away. "What peculiar eyes…"

"Tori," Kincaid interrupts, jutting his chin in the direction of the beaded curtain. "Can we talk?"

Tori blinks and then deflates, her face crumpling as she looks away from me. "Of course."

Kincaid gives a look that says to behave without the need for words and then stalks through the curtain.

"Feel free to have a look around," Tori calls back to me as she follows Kincaid. "Just mind the dolls. They bite. Oh! And don't open any of those boxes over there, 'kay?"

A cold fist closes around my heart.

I give the strange woman a nod, wanting to tell her not to worry because I won't be touching a damn thing in this place.

Tori's Oddities? More like Tori's demon possessed playthings.

I shiver and wrap my arms around myself, wishing I'd pulled one of the new sweaters I bought over my gross top. Despite myself, I can't help the urge to at least *look* at all the strange and foreign things in the shop, though I stick as near to the glass beaded curtain as I can, not wanting to stray too far lest I be lost in the maze of oddities or crushed by a tower of books.

Or, you know, bitten by a demonic fucking doll.

Hurry up, Kincaid, I urge him in my mind, squealing when I accidentally bump into a low table and knock several inked maps from its surface.

I jerk my gaze to the beaded curtain, half expecting Kincaid to come thundering out and drag me from the shop. He doesn't. Righting the maps, I notice one of St. Louis.

Well, of what *used* to be St. Louis.

It's a map of Elisium. Hand drawn after the city fell. Maybe not so long ago.

It shows The Hinge and the demon market. There are several other landmarks I don't recognize. A bath-house and a hotel called The Red Lion.

Some place called the Midnight Court.

And many others.

Impulsively, I roll the map and tuck it into my back pocket. Something like this could come in handy.

The crinkle of the parchment paper as I walk sets my teeth on edge. I don't go far, but I give the doll case a wide berth. Ignoring that there are not one, but several sets of eyes following me as I go.

I still as a muffled whisper brushes past my ears then whirl searching for the source. "Hello?" I whisper into the dim, the hairs on the back of my neck standing on end.

Silence.

Then it starts again. More than one voice this time. A barrage of indeterminable whispers making word sounds but absolutely no sense.

Impulsively, I reach for my wrist, to twist the beads of my bracelets, but find only bare skin, and instead I bite my lower lip.

"Kincaid?" I call tentatively, my heart in my throat as I walk backward the way I came, searching the shadows and piles of junk for the faces of monsters. Nothing moves.

There's no one else here.

There's no one else here.

I force myself to stop. To be braver.

Buck up, Paige.

How the hell do you expect to get your sorry ass home if you can't even face some ominous whispering?

Before I can change my mind, I charge forward, past the doll case, past the table filled with little boxes whose lids are not to be removed, and around a rack of capes, searching for the voice.

It seems to be coming from all directions, but mostly this one. The whispers grow louder with each step, and it takes everything inside of me not to cover my ears and crouch into a tiny ball on the floor and wait for Kincaid to take me away from here.

That's when I see it.

I don't know how I know it's where the whispers are coming from. I just do.

The staff stands alone, with nothing holding it up even though the heavy-looking top of it should make it fall. Twin horns curl outward from a knobby pointed tip. In its slim base, I make out the rough shapes of runes carved into the black wood.

It looks like something an evil wizard would use. Like it could belong to Saruman. Like it belongs in a place like Middle Earth. Or you know…*Hell.*

The whispers seem to be trying to tell me something, but I don't know what.

"I—I don't understand," I croak, my voice breaking. The whispers do not change or cease. I can't understand them. But the more they whisper, the more I am drawn to it.

My mind wanders into a fog.

A weight on my chest quickly grows into a crushing pressure that steals the breath from my lungs and leaves me gasping. Sweat beads at my hairline.

I know this feeling, I realize. I've felt it before.

My fingers reach out. I need to touch it.

I need to…

All at once, the whispers stop.

The pressure is lifted and a breath so deep and sharp it sends my body into a convulsion fills my lungs.

Strong hands come around my arms from behind, and I scream, lashing out, trying to get free.

"Na'vazēm!"

I stop struggling, distantly recognizing that it's Kincaid. When he releases me, I fall back, off-balance and breathless into his chest. The sharp scents of hickory and musk snap me out of the daze.

Kincaid awkwardly shuffles me away from the warmth of his body, holding me steady with one hand until I can regain my footing. I am grateful and eager to move away from him.

As soon as the black spots in my vision dissipate, I do.

"Na'vazēm, what happened?" he demands in a growl.

Tori appears at his side and emits an exclamation when she sees me. I wonder if I look as bad as I feel.

"Is she ill?" Tori asks.

"I—I'll get her a tonic," she adds before Kincaid can answer and vanishes back through the maze of oddities.

"I said *what happened?*"

I can't stop staring at the staff. My mouth is dry, and my throat feels like it's full of sand. The whispers…

They're all gone.

I hear nothing save for the raucous bleating of my own heart fighting to find the dregs of oxygen still in my system and pump them to my brain.

"It whispered," I hear myself say, barely recognizing my own voice.

Kincaid follows my line of sight to the horned staff and his grip on my arm tightens.

"Tori," he bellows.

I recoil from the fury in his tone, even though it isn't directed at me. He lets me jerk my arm free of his grasp, and I stumble two steps back until I knock into a table, gripping the edge of it to steady myself.

She appears only a couple seconds later, a clay mug in her hands. She looks at Kincaid askance as she holds out the mug to me. "Drink," she orders. "You're depleted, this will replenish—"

"Where did you get this?" Kincaid hisses at her.

I take the mug from Tori, if only so she'll stop holding it so close to my face and sniff the fizzing liquid inside. It smells like sweet wine.

Lifting it to my lips, I take a tiny sip, wetting my tongue with the sweet, slightly-acrid nectar. It tastes nothing like it smells, but it isn't awful. I gulp another small mouthful.

"A seller brought it in about a week ago," Tori explains, her ashen skin seeming to pale even more. "Said it was forged in the fires of Hell."

Kincaid is staring at the staff like he might recognize it. I notice how his fists are clenched at his sides. And how the skin of his fingers seems to be blackening. The inky tone slowly creeping up his fingers to claim his knuckles.

I'd only half believed the thing in the park that night was Kincaid. That dark-skinned *thing* with the tail and horns. It really was him, though. A ball forms in my throat and a cool sweat pricks at my chest. I take another step away from him, trying to be sly about it.

Please don't turn into a monster. Please don't turn into a monster.

"Seems the seller was right," Tori says with a smirk when Kincaid doesn't reply, some color returning to her cheeks. "How about that…"

Kincaid cuts his yellow gaze to me and my teeth clench. Then he looks back to the staff, a knot forming between his brows.

"We'll take the staff," he tells Tori, but doesn't make any move to grab hold of it. I certainly wouldn't want to touch the thing, either, and I'm not too happy with the idea of it coming home with us.

"I didn't say it was for sale."

Kincaid glares at her, his nostrils flaring.

She lifts her hands in a placating gesture and grins. "Okay, okay. Calm down, oh powerful one. I suppose it can be sold. For the right price."

"What do you want for it?"

Tori seems to consider, tapping two fingers against her chin.

I sip more of the weird drink, feeling less sluggish and more alert with each sip.

"A lord's pardon," she finally decides. "Should I ever end up…you know where…I think I'd like a way out."

"You know I can't do that," Kincaid growls at her.

She merely grins in reply. "Yes," she says, a challenge in her tone. "You can."

I swear I can almost hear his teeth grinding with each flare of his cheekbones.

"I could just take it, you know," Kincaid warns, pivoting a step toward the gravity defying staff.

Tori crosses her arms. Clucks her tongue. "But you won't."

I like her.

Visibly deflating, Kincaid sneers at her. "Twenty thousand," he offers her.

She shakes her head.

"Twenty-*five* thousand," he amends.

"Nope," she replies with an audible pop of her lips.

"*Fine*," Kincaid all but shouts. "Pack it up."

"I want you to say it."

Kincaid closes the small gap between himself and Tori, his massive frame hulking over her, but she is not cowed. Somehow, she doesn't even seem afraid. "I, Asmodeus, Lord of Hell, hereby grant you a way out of Hell should you ever find yourself in need of one. There. *Satisfied?*"

No.

No, no, no.

Nope.

I stare incredulously at Kincaid. Or should I call him Asmodeus?

Lord of fucking Hell?

What even is that?

I've never heard of such a thing. This is so bad. This is so much worse than I ever thought it could be.

I made a bargain with a *lord of Hell?*

Tori's bright white teeth flash in a full smile, offset by the rich tone of her skin. "*Very* satisfied."

"Now," Kincaid hisses. "Pack. It. Up."

"With pleasure, Mr. Kincaid."

Tori does a little curtsey that I think is more a mockery than anything and rushes away. She returns with something that looks like a blanket only a few seconds later. It's a stiff, dark gray material. She sets to wrapping the staff with it, and I don't miss how she is cautious *not* to touch it.

"You said it whispered," Kincaid says, his attention turned back to me, and even though he hasn't edged the words in a question, I can tell he expects an answer.

I lower my gaze, not wanting to look at him for

KISS OF THE DAMNED

another second. "Yes. Or at least, I think it was the staff."

His jaw tightens.

"Can you hear it now?"

I part my lips to reply. To tell him no, but that's not quite true. Distantly, I realize, I can still hear them. Though they are so faint, it's almost as though they aren't there at all.

"I think so. It's…distant."

His lips press into a firm line.

"Wait, can you *not* hear them?"

"No, *Na'vazēm.* I cannot."

An anvil drops in my gut.

"What does that mean?"

He doesn't answer.

"Kincaid, what does that—"

He holds up a hand to silence me, and my stomach turns.

Tori loops a small bit of thin silvery rope around the base of the staff, coiling it upward and then tying it off at the top. When she steps back from the thing, it somehow still stands.

I don't like it.

"Do we have to take that thing back to the house?" I grouse, my voice small and barely above a whisper.

When Kincaid doesn't respond, Tori gives me a tight smile and puts her hands on her hips, changing the direction of the conversation. "So," she says cheerfully, looking between mine and Kincaid's grim faces.

151

"Will I be seeing you lot at the Court of Nightmares on the next moon?"

"I'll be there," Kincaid grunts.

Tori turns her bright violet eyes toward me. "Hope you'll bring your new friend."

"No."

"A shame," Tori says with a pout. "They'd eat up a pretty thing like her."

Kincaid visibly stiffens then moves forward in a blur of speed to snatch up the staff, snagging my hand as he storms back the way he came, jostling me.

The mug falls to the floor, shattering against the threadbare carpet. The sweet liquid steams lightly when it makes contact.

"I—I'm sorry," I call back to Tori as Kincaid drags me back through the maze of oddities to the front door.

"No worries, love!" she hollers back. "You can pay for the mug *and* the map next time."

Tori winks at me, and my mouth snaps shut as Kincaid pulls me out of sight.

Tori's voice calls to us as Kincaid kicks open the front door and yanks me outside, "Come again soon!"

🎐 17 🎐

Here lies Paige Marie St. Clare.

The biggest idiot of all time.

That's what my headstone will say. After this *demon* kills me.

I eye Kincaid sitting across from me at the table. Neither of us spoke after he chucked the staff into the front seat next to his chauffeur and herded me into the backseat.

We didn't speak when we arrived back at the house.

Not when I gathered up all my shopping bags and rushed upstairs to the room he assigned me.

He didn't come up when I had my second shower-bath of the day. Or when I stayed up there for over an hour numbly getting dressed, uncovering ornate furniture, and putting away the clothes he bought for me.

I only left the room at all because I was hungry.

Now here we are.

Me, with a plate of buttered and salted noodles I scavenged from the grand galley kitchen. The demon slouches in a high-backed chair at the other end of the table, a silver goblet dangling from his fingers. He swirls the liquid inside, watching me with a predator's gaze.

The pasta sits heavily in my stomach, and I find I'm nearly full after only a couple of bites.

"I suppose you have questions," he says, finishing off the last dregs of his drink and refilling the goblet from a carafe atop the table. His yellow eyes burn into me. His head tilts to one side.

I clear my throat, shoving the plate away.

"Are you really—"

"One of the seven lords of Hell?" he interrupts. "Yes. Anything else?"

My body goes cold at the stark, humorless admission. My mouth is sandpaper dry.

"Okay," I manage, folding my fingers together in my lap.

"*Okay?*" he presses, a curious lilt to the word.

I nod, pressing my lips together.

I mean, it makes sense now. Why all the whispering at the demon market. Why everyone seemed to let him do whatever the hell he wanted. Why no one wanted to get in his way.

Except Tori.

"Tori, what was she?" I ask, more out of curiosity than anything. I wonder if she is also a being of great power. She didn't back down from Kincaid. She didn't cower like the rest.

I envy her that.

Kincaid seems taken by surprise at the direction of my questions. "A gargoyle," he replies without elaborating.

"A gargoyle? Like the creepy statue things on churches?"

"They have a more ancient name, but they adopted the moniker a couple hundred years ago. It was fitting."

"Fitting how?"

He narrows his eyes. I can tell he's more than a little annoyed to have to be answering my questions, but I can't seem to help myself. I want to know.

I want to know *everything*.

All of it.

"Have you never heard of her kind? I assumed all mortals on the other side of The Hinge would be well versed in all things Diablim by now."

I swallow. "Not me."

Though I may have heard the name before, I likely dismissed it. After all, a gargoyle was a made-up thing. A monstrous beast thought to scare away evil spirits from places of worship. They aren't real.

Tori definitely didn't have fangs or wings or claws.

Kincaid sighs. "They're hard as stone. Their skin is all but impenetrable by mortal or demon-forged weapons," he tells me then grimaces. "And they can't be swayed by powers of the mind."

Sounds pretty freaking great. Why couldn't I have been a gargoyle?

Or maybe I am. Who freaking knows at this point.

"Sounds pretty amazing."

He nods.

"They are. And rare. Even more rare for one to live in Elisium. They're Nephilim."

My eyes go wide at that.

I suppose I shouldn't be surprised. I know lots of Nephilim live in Elisium. But unlike what I assumed—that the Nephilim were here to help control and contain the Diablim—Tori lives among them.

She runs a shop filled with demonic oddities. She buys from Diablim and sells to demons.

I'm not sure what to make of it. What little I thought I knew about the world outside Ford's door is being tested. The contents of my mind shaken and shredded.

"It's my turn," Kincaid says after a moment, rising to procure a second goblet from a buffet and hutch pressed against the wall next to the long table. He fills it from the carafe and lifts his own, coming to set the newly filled goblet down in front of me.

A peace offering?

I don't take it.

He sits on the table's ledge like he did this morning at breakfast, his stare penetrating. Calculated.

"How is it that you were able to live on the mortal

side of The Hinge without being discovered for so long?"

A vivid image of Ford flashes beneath my eyelids when I drop my head and squeeze them tight. I don't want to talk about that.

I don't ever want to think about it again.

The nightmares are enough of a reminder. I don't need to relive it in the light of day, too.

"You said someone named Ford kept you locked up, but you didn't finish. Who is this *Ford*? What do you mean by 'locked up?'"

My body is so tense it feels like all my muscles are only seconds from tearing. My stomach roils and the bitter taste of acid coats my tongue.

I don't realize I'm shaking my head until Kincaid slips from the table's ledge and kneels next to my chair. I jerk back from him, the images of Ford in my mind making me extra edgy.

I have to remind myself he's dead several times to calm down.

For a second, I think Kincaid might reach out to me. There's a sadness pulling at the corners of his eyes as he searches mine. Then the second passes and his regular stoic impassiveness is firmly back in place.

A warm pull tingles low in my belly, and suddenly, I can't look away from his warm honey and sunshine eyes. They're so beautiful.

They're unlike anything I've ever seen before.

Distantly, I know something is wrong. As my body

shudders from the power he's exerting over me with his mind, I know the sensations fluttering over the surface of my skin, making my thighs clench, aren't real.

In a daze, I lean forward, eager to touch him. Wanting to feel the roughness of the light stubble at his chin. Wishing he would touch me, not just with his mind, but with those long fingers of his.

I wonder if his raven black hair is as soft as it looks.

I squirm in my seat, my body as pliable as soft clay.

Kincaid stops me before I can get near enough to touch him. He holds me at arms-length, and his smell, that spicy hickory and vanilla musk, makes me moan, wanting to get closer. Wanting to breathe it in more deeply. To taste it.

"Tell me," he demands, and the press and pull of his demonic magic wanes just a little. "What did he do to you?"

Without the awful memories and the tension they bring, it seems the easiest thing in the world to tell him. It doesn't matter anymore. That part of my life is over.

Maybe if I tell Kincaid, he'll be happy. Maybe he'll stop holding me at arms-length.

I'd like that.

I'd like to make him happy.

"He was a bad man," I slur.

Kincaid waits for more.

I give it to him.

I tell him how I've left the security of Ford's house

less times than I can count on two hands. I tell him about the dead room. The smell of the dead things he locked inside it with me.

How they were never quite dead.

How even though they were stiff with rigor mortis or missing entire sections of skin, revealing white bone, they would come back to life.

"They were demonic," I tell Kincaid without emotion. "And when they came back to life, he would shock me. Sometimes with the chair. Sometimes with the rod."

I tell him how I think Ford was trying to make me afraid to leave. I tell him how it mostly worked. I don't glaze over anything. He's so easy to talk to. It feels good to get it all out.

The words leave my lips in a deluge of a thousand stories rushing to be heard. They tumble forth without a care. Like they aren't the worst words in the whole world.

Kincaid learns about the tracker I was forced to wear. About the false claims of my insanity, though I do mention that perhaps I am insane. I haven't ruled that out.

He learns of the hose. How the pressure of its icy water peeled back skin on more than one occasion.

And all the while he looks angrier. I'm confused because didn't he want to know? I thought knowing would make him happy, and I wanted to make him happy, but now I think I've made him angry, and I don't like that.

I don't like it at all.

I stop talking.

"I'm sorry," I whisper. "Now I've made you angry. I didn't want to make you angry."

Kincaid looks at me like he's seeing me for the first time. In awe, but also so filled with rage it takes my breath away. I want to smooth the wrinkles in his forehead. I want to erase the tension around his mouth with a kiss pressed to his lips.

He releases his hold on me, both physically and mentally, and stands.

It's like there's been an elastic band pulled tight around me, and the instant he moves away, it *snaps*. I'm catapulted back to myself.

I blink fast, still shivering from the aftereffects of his power over my desire. My sex throbs beneath my clothes, and my fingernails dig into the distressed wood of my chair's armrests.

"No," he says in a faraway voice, as if he isn't even aware he's spoken.

He goes to walk away, and with the sudden clarity comes a fury so hot and so harrowing that I begin to shake.

My chair falls back when I rise on shaking legs.

Unthinking, I lunge for him.

I've never been violated like he's just violated me.

He didn't touch me, sure. But he altered my mind.

Reached his long-fingered hands inside of me and forced me to tell him my secrets. My nightmarish truths.

I've never thrown a punch in my life, but I do now. My fingers curl in of their own accord. I reel back and swing.

Kincaid doesn't move out of the way, even though in my red-tinted vision it's clear he sees the strike coming a mile away. His jaw barely registers my blow, jarring slightly to one side at the impact of my white-knuckled fist.

I cry out, clutching my hand to my chest with a hissing groan.

"Damnit!" I shout, rubbing my throbbing knuckles and wondering distantly if I broke my thumb.

"Damn *you!*" I seethe, setting my gaze on him and hoping it conveys the depths of my rage.

Kincaid, wholly unaffected by my blow, stares openly at me. Something I can't name in his eyes. He doesn't say a word.

"Don't stare at me like that!" I hiss at him, and a strange fraying sensation pulls at my edges. Something cold and heavy worms into my chest.

He stares.

Snarling like some kind of animal, I shove him, needing him to stop looking at me like that. I can't stand it.

I'm beginning to unravel, and I *hate* it. My rage is making way for something far more dangerous. My throat scratches and my eyes burn. I shove him again and again.

It only makes me angrier that he won't move. He won't fall. He won't fucking fight back. I want him to be the monster I know he is.

Why won't he defend himself?

The tears are coming now and there's no stopping them. I'll be *damned* if I let him see me cry. I won't give him the satisfaction of knowing how thoroughly he's undone me.

Gathering up the last bit of untainted fury I have in my bones, I pull back from him and stare straight into his stupid yellow eyes.

"You're a *monster*," I rasp and rush from the room before the first tear can fall.

❧ 18 ❧

I am an idiot.

The tears on my pillow have dried and yesterday's blazing fury has turned to ash in my mouth. I meant what I said. I *hate* Kincaid. I already hated him. For being what he is. For purchasing me like I'm some *item* to be bought. For locking me away and trying to starve me.

It's more than that now, though. Those other transgressions seem far away. I hadn't forgiven him his trespasses, but I'd let them go, contented by the protection of the bargain we struck.

Last night Kincaid reminded me just how foolish it was to do that. I did the one thing I told myself I wouldn't do. I dropped my guard. I got *comfortable* with a demon.

It sounds like an oxymoron, like it's impossible, but there it is.

That wasn't even my biggest mistake. I can hardly believe I shouted at him and shoved him.

For the tenth time since I woke, I drop my head and press the heels of my hands into my eyes, as if I can erase the events of the night before if I just press hard enough.

I punched a demon in the face.

No. Scratch that. I punched a *lord of Hell* in the face.

Surely there was going to be repercussions for that, and I have no one to blame my own damn self. How could I be so stupid?

I should know better.

Though, even now, there is a lick of fury still simmering just below the surface of my regret, and it whispers how he deserved it. It whispers that I shouldn't be sorry.

It's a small part of me that still has the courage to be defiant. I thought I killed it a long time ago, but there it is, rearing its ugly head. It's going to get me killed.

A double rap at my door makes me jerk my hands away from my face. My pulse skitters and a bolt of icy heat darts down my back, forcing my spine erect.

"Yes?" I croak, not daring to move. Hardly able to breathe.

I picture him there on the other side of the door. With an angry sneer and his fists ready to punish. What methods will he use to torture me?

"*Uh,*" comes a voice that is decidedly *not* Kincaid.

"Miss? My name is Artemis. Master Kincaid purchased me from—"

I am on my feet and ripping the door nearly from its hinges with sloppy fingers. Before me in the hallway is the boy from the back of the van. The Nephilim boy who healed me. He reels back from me as though I might attack him at first but then just raises a brow. "Oh," he says oddly with a strange little grin. "It's you."

Words escape me. I'm not sure what to say or what this means. Even after I attacked him, Kincaid made good on his end of the bargain.

I open and close my mouth several times before remembering how to speak. "You're here."

He narrows his bright blue eyes at me, his hair, somehow even more matted and ratty than before covers most of his forehead and part of his eyes. "The demon lord, he said you bargained for me."

I grin and nod.

"I did."

The boy fixes me with an incredulous look. "*So*," he says, drawing out the 'o' sound in a way that drips with sarcasm. "You bargained to have me bought by the biggest, baddest demon in Elisium?"

I open my mouth, but no words come out.

I'd been trying to help him. I wanted to get him away from those awful Diablim women so I could... could what? Protect him?

"You made me the property of a lord of Hell to...*help me?*"

"Well, I—" I stammer, but the boy cuts me off with a laugh. A deep, hoarse laugh that starts low in his belly and morphs into a raucous, foot-stomping howl. He presses a hand to his gut as though the force of his laughter hurts. Twin tears carve clean paths through the grime streaking his cheeks.

He lifts a blackened and bloodstained finger to wipe one away, smearing his temple with re-wetted blood. "Oh man!" he says between fits of laughter. "That's—I don't even know what that is."

"Look, maybe I can—"

He shakes his head and steps forward to pat me on my unbandaged shoulder. "At least this'll be more interesting," he says, still wheezing from laughter. "Maybe I'll get to die epically, instead of on the side-lines of a fighting pit at The Freakshow."

The...*what?*

The boy nudges past me into my room. "You got a bathroom?" he asks, taking in the space. Then he seems to realize something and pauses. "Wait..." he trails off. "Does Master Kincaid let you stay in this room?"

He whirls with an unreadable expression on his youthful, tarnished face.

"He does."

The boy's shoulders sag a little, and he looks like someone's just smacked him upside the head. His eyes widen and he almost staggers. "Huh," he says, blinking at me before his stare turns accusing. "I think maybe I underestimated you."

I cross my arms, wincing when my shoulder injury smarts at the movement.

"Maybe you did," I say, trying to seem more confident than I feel.

I can't promise this boy I'll save him, but I wish I could tell him my plan is to bring him back across The Hinge with me because that's exactly what I intend to do. Instead I'm silently cursing myself that I didn't also bargain for *his* freedom, only that Kincaid would bring him here.

See? Idiot.

"Who exactly are you? *What* are you?"

"Paige," I tell him. "And I don't know what I am."

His thin brows lift at that, but he makes no comment.

"Artemis," he replies, and extends a hand. He can't be more than thirteen, but he's nearly as tall as I am already. Only half a head shorter. I shake his hand, unperturbed by the bloodied, dirty state of them.

He makes no secret of studying my eyes. For once though, I do not turn away.

His mouth puckers as though he's considering something very seriously. "There a shower in there?" he asks, jabbing a thumb in the direction of the bathroom.

I nod.

He looks like he's ready to cry with relief, and I wonder when the last time was that he was permitted to bathe. He inhales shakily and grins. "When I'm finished, I'll take care of that for you," he says with a nudge of his chin in the direction of my still-bandaged shoulder.

"You don't have to."

He holds up a hand. "If you can get me something to eat, I'll heal every tiny scratch you got."

"That's not why I brought you here," I argue. "I just wanted to help—"

"I know," he interrupts, a seriousness deepening his pre-pubescent voice. There's a hardness in his luminous blue eyes that no boy his age should possess. I see a likeness in him. A shared understanding of the darkness.

We are the same, I realize. That's why I felt the urge to try to save him before this broken world could twist him beyond repair. Like it twisted me.

"I know that," he repeats. "But I want to."

❧ 19 ❧

I t takes me only a moment to draw up the courage to go downstairs and find Artemis something to eat.

Whereas I'd meandered in my room for hours this morning, too afraid to venture out, I'm emboldened by Artemis' presence. The weight of his being here rests heavily on my shoulders. Inadvertently, I've made him my responsibility.

I brought him here, to the lion's den, and now it's my job to see he escapes it unscathed. Leaving this room to quell the hunger in my own stomach wasn't worth it, but the boy asked me for food and the least I can do is oblige him. Especially after I just dragged him from one hellhole to another possibly more dangerous one.

Grumbling quietly to myself, I make my way

through the house, ears straining for sound and heart fluttering.

Please don't be home.

Please don't be home.

A throat clears behind me only a second after I've entered the kitchen. I stop in my tracks, shoulders stiffening.

"*Na'vazēm,*" he says in a voice that manages to be both rumbling and soft.

I turn, cautiously peeking at his expression while also judging the distance between where I stand and the exit on the other end of the galley kitchen. There are only two ways out and Kincaid is blocking the other.

His expression, unsurprisingly, is unreadable, as it so often is. I can't tell from a look in his eyes what his intentions are like I could Ford. I truly don't know.

I try to form the words for an apology, but that stubborn pocket of defiant fury is still there, and I can't say it. It would be a lie. Was it true that demons could tell if you were lying?

"Thank you," I say instead, and even that tastes foul on my tongue. "For bringing the boy."

"It was part of our bargain."

"Right."

Kincaid licks his lips, and something slithers through my belly in response. I worry for a moment that he's using his ability on me again, but he isn't looking at me. His gaze is downcast as he runs a shaky hand through his tousled black hair.

He looks more disheveled than I've ever seen him before, I realize. His plain cotton shirt is undone at the top, revealing the smooth expanse of his tan chest beneath. His pants look rumpled, like he might've fallen asleep in them, and his eyes, normally a bright almost radiant yellow gold are dull and so bloodshot I have to wonder if he even slept at all.

"Are you sick?" The question topples from my lips, and I'm taken aback at how worried it sounds when it does. I bite my tongue to keep anything else from coming out.

He crooks his neck to stare at me curiously. "No," he answers and then seems to come back to himself. "No, of course I'm not, don't be ridiculous."

"Okay," I all but snap. "Never mind then."

I turn away, but Kincaid stops me, moving so fast I don't even see him until he's standing in front of me again. Startled, I fall back, knocking into a spice rack on the countertop. Jars rattle and fall, rolling from the counter's edge.

I fumble to catch them before they can shatter, but Kincaid is faster, snatching all three up in the span of a single blink and then placing them slowly back on the counter.

"I didn't come to you to trade insults."

"Then what do you want?"

This time, I *can* tell he's angry. A vein jumps in his left temple when his jaw clenches. "For you to fulfill your end. There's somewhere I want to take you. Tonight."

"Where?"

"Bellefontaine," he says, as if I should know what that means. "If I'm right about what I think you are, it won't be pleasant."

I huff a vicious laugh. He clearly wasn't hearing me when he made me spill my entire life's sob story to him last night. He doesn't need to warn me, since when is anything ever pleasant in the life of Paige St. Clare?

"What time?"

"At three."

"I thought you said tonight?"

It would be three in less than two hours from now.

"Three in the morning. We'll leave just before then."

Lovely.

"Is that all?" I ask as tonelessly as I am able, trying to hide how incredibly uncomfortable he's making me. His mood swings are giving me whiplash.

"One more thing, I meant to ask before but…" he trails off.

"You mean when you ransacked my head?"

I couldn't help myself.

Kincaid grimaces. "Who are your parents, Paige?"

I'm taken aback at the question. He already knows Ford was my legal guardian. When I don't answer straight away, his eyes glint with the bitter edge of rancor.

Not wanting him to do what he did last night *again*, I tell him. It's no secret. "I don't know," I state matter-of-factly. "My mom's name was Cassandra St. Clare. As far as I know she was mortal. She was raped—*apparently* by a Diablim—and I am the result. That's all I know."

It's all Ford would tell me about her. A hollowness spreads like poison in my gut.

My fingernails carve half-moons into my palms. I can't meet Kincaid's fiery gaze, but I can feel it on my cheek. "Are we done here?"

Kincaid leaves without replying, but I think I hear him whisper something under his breath. I can't make it out.

Once he's gone, I slump against the counter, glaring at my body as if it's a separate entity from myself.

"Get your shit together, Paige," I hiss, shaking the disquiet from my skull as I rummage for something for Artemis to eat.

I've completely lost my appetite.

I ROLL MY SHOULDER, AMAZED AT ARTEMIS' SKILL. IT'S completely healed. As is what remained of the small cuts on my palms, though those had nearly healed themselves already.

Both Artemis and I had been surprised to find the wound in my shoulder had mostly healed itself, too. After I'd explained to him what happened and how deep the punctures were—well, suffice it to say, he was confused when the bandage came off.

The three puncture marks were fully closed and scabbed over.

"Don't look so impressed," Artemis said around a mouthful of canned beans. I really needed to ask Kincaid to stock the kitchen better. Besides canned goods and shelf stable items, there wasn't much at all. The fridge stood all but empty, with a funny smell inside. And the breadbox held nothing but a loaf of old bread, covered over in fuzzy blue mold.

Did demons not eat?

"There was barely anything left for me to heal," he continues after a big swallow.

Artemis practically glows after his long shower earlier in the day. His hair is still a little matted, and I expect he'll need a fine-tooth comb to get the small dreads out of it, or maybe a haircut, but his muddy-brown hair looks more like shiny milk chocolate now. And I never would have guessed there was a smattering of light freckles beneath all the grime coating his cheeks.

He looks exactly like someone who does *not* belong in Elisium.

"When did you say that happened to your shoulder?"

I work to remember. I've begun counting the days since Kincaid and my bargain was struck. Only 38 more until I'll gain my freedom. Which means the run in with the daeva in the park was... "About four days ago. Maybe five. I was passed out for a while."

He frowns. "That's some speedy healing. Guess you really are Diablim then. Maybe close to a pure blood."

"Do they heal faster than others?"

He nods. "Yeah. Demons heal the fastest. Like, lightning fast. Pure-blooded Diablim heal really fast. Low level Diablim still heal faster than a mortal, but not by much."

Curiosity piqued, I tug my sleeve back on and cross my legs atop the bed. "And Nephilim?"

He makes a so-so motion with his head, his mouth filled again with beans. "Pretty much the same."

I remember the books downstairs in the library. Part of the bargain with Kincaid allows me to read them, but with everything going on, all of it happening so fast, the desire for knowledge has taken a back seat to other more pressing issues.

"Hey," I say, jumping up from the bed. Artemis snatches up his bowl to keep it from spilling as the whole thing is jostled. "Have you heard of Bellefontaine?"

The little drawer on the left side of the vanity squeals as I pull it open and retrieve the map I snatched from Tori's shop. It crinkles as I splay it open in front of Artemis on the bed.

"Yeah," Artemis says, glancing curiously at the map of Elisium. I can tell he's wondering where I got it, but he doesn't ask.

"It's a cemetery," he tells me, pointing at a spot on the map that's all the way on the other side of the city. "Why is he taking you there?"

My nose wrinkles as though the scent of death already clogs my nostrils. My lungs seize and despite myself, my bottom lip trembles.

"Hey, are you okay?" Artemis asks me, his bowl of beans forgotten for the moment.

I shake my head, more to clear it than to give an answer. "No—I mean, yes. Yes, I'm fine."

"You sure? You went all green for a second."

I take a few deep breaths to center myself and reroll the map, tucking it back where I got it from on legs that feel suddenly weak.

Of course he's taking me to a cemetery.

Bastard.

Tiny fragments of memories turn into clues in my mind. I struggle to string them together, but the picture they form is discordant and marred. And it isn't one I like.

Ford liked to torture me with dead things, too. Why should Kincaid be any different?

Except…I thought maybe he was.

"Who's that?" Artemis asks, and I turn to follow his gaze to the open bedroom door. Sitting squarely in the middle, tail swishing back and forth, is Kincaid's cat.

Even from here, I can hear it purr softly as it watches us with bright green eyes. For the first time, I notice how strange they are. There's no discernible pupil. The entire oculus is just solid green.

"A demonic cat," I say, backing away a step when the feline lifts itself and slinks into the room.

"No way!" Artemis exclaims cheerfully. "I didn't know there were demon cats. Hellhounds, sure. But not *cats*."

"*Shoo*," I tell it, trying to make a brushing motion with my hands that I hope scares it enough to leave but not enough to attack.

It mistakes my attempt as a call for it to come and patters over to me, it's little belled collar chiming. Even as I back away until I'm blocked by the bed, it comes. It sits at my feet, curling its tail around its body as it stares up at me.

Meowing loudly, it cocks its demonic little head.

"Awe, look," Artemis says. "It likes you."

I don't like it, but I think maybe the boy is right. After a moment of watching me, perhaps checking to make sure I'm not going to step on its tail again, it brushes its little nose and flat forehead against my shin, beginning to purr again.

Tentatively, I lower myself, not making any sudden movements.

What was it they said in all those nature documentaries. You need to let the animal scent you before touching it? Taking a chance, I put my hand out to the cat and wait while it sniffs my fingertips for a second before pushing its little head into my hand.

I pet it, reveling in the softness of its fur. This time when I find its little horns buried beneath, I don't freak out. I finger their ridged edges and grin. "You aren't so scary," I tell it. "It's not your fault you're a demon cat."

I giggle when it bumps its cold little nose to my palm. "What's your name?" I ask it as though I'm anticipating an answer and feel under its chin for the collar.

There's a name tag next to the little bell, but it's blank.

"Don't tell me Kincaid didn't bother naming you? How rude."

Artemis slides from the bed to his knees, reaching out a hand for the cat to acquaint itself to him.

At this angle, with what remains of the daylight streaming in from the window, there's a strange, other-worldly glow around Artemis. I see it come in a flash, glowing like the purest form of radiant light in his bright blue eyes when he grins up at me, and the cat strides cautiously to him.

And then it's gone just as quickly as it came.

The cat takes one sniff of Artemis and makes a swipe at his hand. Raising its back impossibly high, it hisses at him and then rushes away, pausing to hiss one more time before it vanishes.

Artemis shrugs. "Figures."

I consider the Nephilim boy for a moment. Surprised at the strange feeling taking root in my gut. Like if the cat doesn't trust him, then maybe I shouldn't either. I mean, I'm fairly certain he just *glowed* a second ago, so…

He catches me staring and smirks. "Angel-born," he says, pointing at himself.

"Demon cat," he says, pointing out the door. "We don't exactly get along."

"Right."

I slump, wondering if that was the glow I saw. Something to do with his being Nephilim…but no, that couldn't be it. The diviner who effectively destroyed my life didn't glow.

Ugh. Who knows? Maybe I'm just finally losing my mind.

It'd be about time.

❧ 2 0 ❧

When I leave my room just before three in the morning, exhausted but also somehow more alert than I've ever been, I can tell Kincaid is already waiting for me.

I creep on tiptoe past the door next to my room. Artemis snores softly within, and I don't want to wake him. The space was vacant and when day turned to night and he began to yawn, I thought we should find some place for him to sleep.

I wouldn't have been opposed to sharing my bed, but I was *not* the ideal sleeping companion. Waking often from nightmares and tossing and turning at all hours. I'd give my left kidney to have my weighted blanket back.

I hoped Kincaid wouldn't be angry that I'd taken it upon myself to assign him his own room, too. Kincaid was nowhere to be found to ask first.

37 days, I remind myself. Just 37 more days.

It's taken me until today to fully realize the potential of my freedom and what it could mean. I'd always pictured it like a fragile thing. I'd envisioned myself in a cabin in the woods away from people—from their illnesses that could kill me.

That picture has since changed. Artemis has assured me now for a second time that I am not in any way shape or form *ill.* I never was. I won't ever be.

The possibilities for my freedom lie before me like a runway and I'm eager to take flight.

Except...

I am not mortal.

No matter how many times I think it, it doesn't seem any more true, but there it is. And who is to say that even if Kincaid does return me to the mortal side of The Hinge that the people there won't throw me back like an unwanted fish from a hooked line?

As I pad down the stairs, Kincaid's yellow eyes shine when he lifts them to me, and I smooth the worried knot from my brow. He seems to consider me from head to toe, and I cringe as though I can feel everywhere his eyes touch.

Wordlessly, he lifts a black jacket from a hook above a round receptacle full of umbrellas and canes and hands it to me as I approach. "You'll be wanting something warmer."

I realize I'm still in the shorts from earlier and the most comfortable t-shirt I could find in all the clothes stuffed in the dresser. I hadn't even thought I might need to change. It's warm in the house, and I'm not exactly accustomed to going outside.

"I'll just go change," I offer, not wanting to take the jacket, but Kincaid shakes his head.

"There isn't time."

Grudgingly, I take the proffered jacket and slip my arms into the wide sleeves. I hate how when his warm scent of hickory and musk reaches my nose my body tingles all over.

Whatever he did to me the other night—whatever power he has over my desire—must have a lasting effect.

Kincaid nods approvingly, and we leave, boots crunching over the gravel drive toward the gangstermobile.

There's no driver tonight, I notice as Kincaid slips into the driver's side and grumbles a flustered, "*Get in*," when I hesitate.

I do as I'm told, buckling my seatbelt.

"What did you say?" I ask Kincaid. He'd spoken, but I hadn't heard him.

He starts the car and regards me coolly. "I didn't say anything."

His gaze darts to the backseat for a second, and I whirl to find the staff from Tori's shop laid out across the backseat, partially unwrapped from its silver-threaded gray blanket.

My heart stammers, and I grip the seat beneath me

as if it's a floatation device and this plane is going *down*.

The *rip* of fabric is only background noise to the ever-rising tide of whispers clotting the air in the car. They press in on me, crushing my chest and my windpipe. Trying to suffocate me.

Kincaid exclaims something that sounds like a curse and peels my fingers from the seat where chunky, yellowed foam is spilling out from beneath the leather.

"C-cover it," I beg, shivering as a swift chill fills the car, seeming to burrow into my bones. I wrap Kincaid's jacket tighter around myself, convinced I can see the puff of my own breath in the air.

"*Please,*" I croak, moving my icy fingers up to cover my ears, but it doesn't help. The voices aren't coming from the staff, I realize. Not exactly. Maybe the thing is causing them, but they're inside my head.

Kincaid twists in his seat, and I squeeze my eyes shut, readying myself to flee.

I can't do this.

I can't stay in this car—not with those voices whispering unintelligible words so loud I can't hear my own thoughts. Not while they suffocate me.

"There," Kincaid says, and tugs my hands down from my ears, his bright eyes searching mine in the dark. "It's covered."

I'm panting hard, and I can't seem to stop. The boot on my windpipe has lifted, and I suck in air like there isn't enough in the whole world to sustain me.

Kincaid is still holding my hands I realize as the last

of the whispers fade. His thumb brushes over my knuckle, and I pull away, jumping at the sensation.

He searches my eyes. *"Na'vazēm?"*

I nod. "I'm okay."

Hands returned to the wheel, Kincaid visibly relaxes, and from the side, I watch his Adam's apple bob in his throat. "If you were anyone else, I would kill you for doing that to my car."

I barely hear what he's saying. Mouth agape, I silently gasp as his skin, stained inky black up to his elbows begins to return to his normal shade. The dark shade retreats down his arms like wisps of smoke beneath the surface of his skin until it's gone entirely.

"What are you?" I ask him after we've pulled out from the driveway and onto the road. The tension in my shoulders and the roil of acid in my belly has returned, and I need a distraction.

I half expect him not to answer. He hasn't any other time I've asked, but after a beat of silence, he does.

"I think you already know the answer to that question, *Na'vazēm.*"

I wiggle in my seat and unroll my window just an inch to get some air. "You're a lord of Hell."

I try to state it matter-of-factly, like it doesn't scare me. Like Tori did when she saw him in her shop. Instead, it comes out pitchy.

"I know that already. You said you're one of seven of them."

Which is just...*insane.* I don't even think the mortal

world knows about the seven lords of Hell. I've definitely never heard of them.

"Then what's the question?"

I'm not really sure how to ask what I want to know. I know he's a lord of Hell. I know his true name is Asmodeus. What I don't know is what it is he becomes when his skin turns black and he sprouts horns and a tail.

"Never mind," I mutter, thinking maybe it's best not to know.

The city passes us by in a blur of darkness peppered with small pockets of light. For a city that once held over three-hundred-thousand people, it's eerily quiet now that the Diablim have taken it.

There are so many less of them then there ever were of us.

Them, I correct myself, feeling ill at the thought. I am not mortal.

I am the *them* I fear.

I peer at Kincaid and grit my teeth.

If he isn't *them* anymore, then that makes him and me an *us*.

We are Diablim.

I repeat it in a whisper to myself so low I'm certain Kincaid can't hear over the rumble of the ancient engine. "*I am Diablim.*"

No matter how many times I say it to myself, it never feels more right. It never fits.

"How much further?"

"Not long."

My heart spurs into a gallop, and I try to settle myself by counting to three and trying to retreat to my safe place inside. It works, but not as well as it usually does.

Kincaid readjusts himself in his seat. "Have you noticed a difference?" he asks, and I quirk a brow at him, not catching on to his meaning.

"Since you've ceased taking the pills," he clarifies. "You should be noticing a great many changes by now."

I cringe, knowing without the need to ask exactly what he means. It takes me all of a millisecond to tie it all together. I already suspected it was the pills I had to blame.

Or rather, the lack of them.

"I heal faster," I admit. "My head is clearer. It was always like my thoughts had to wade through maple syrup before, but not anymore."

"What else?"

"I think maybe I'm stronger, too. Or, I don't know, maybe that's just because I'm not being starved or tortured anymore."

Kincaid flinches.

It really could be either, but I know that I shouldn't have been able to run quite so far the night the daeva attacked me. Not after eating so little for so long, and certainly not after barely sleeping and all the horror of finding myself on this side of The Hinge. Since I stopped taking my daily doses, I've gradually gained more energy. More alertness. Last night, I even noticed how well I seemed to be able to see in the pitch blackness of my room with the shutters drawn.

Almost like it was daylight.

I had to cover my head with a pillow to sleep.

Kincaid is right, things are changing, and even though I feel better than I ever have before, I can't say I'm pleased to know the diviner was right about me.

"That's good. It means the poison is leaving your system. I'd give it a few more days for it to fully leave your bloodstream."

…giving my Diablim blood the chance to shine.

He doesn't say it, but it's implied.

When the awkward silence falls again, I find myself eager to fill it. Every mile of pavement we chew is making me more on edge and soon, I'm going to be at risk of staging a breakout, which is decidedly against our bargain.

A shuddering breath leaves my body as I speak. "Your cat," I ask, blurting the first thing that comes to mind. "Does it have a name?"

Kincaid smirks, a small laugh at some private joke whispering through his lips. "No, *Na'vazēm*. It does not have a name. It does not need one."

Poor thing, I think, already trying to come up with something suitable. It proves a good distraction.

I think of its white fur and creepy green eyes. Snowflake, maybe? No, doesn't fit. Lily?

I purse my lips, unable to rest on any one option. I

consider character names from my favorite movies and books and silly names like Sir Fluffyface and Mistress Hornhead, but I don't actually know if it's male or female. I'll have to check.

"We're here," Kincaid says and makes a sharp turn onto a new road. This one is darker than the others we'd taken to get here. All the streetlamps are out. Not a single house or building on the right side of the road looks to contain any form of life.

Bellefontaine Graveyard sprawls to the right further up ahead. Tombstones reach their stony fingers toward the heavens. Mausoleums squat like toads farther in, crawling with vines and overgrown with weeds at their doors.

The moon illuminates a wrought iron gate next to where Kincaid parks the car. I can feel his eyes on me, watching me watch the graves.

I wonder if he knows what I'm thinking.

Why I am so afraid.

Did I tell him what Ford did to me in the dead room? I'm fairly certain I did. Except, I'm starting to doubt the reason Ford stuffed dead animals into the cramped space with me. I don't think it was to frighten me off leaving.

I don't understand how I can be so sure, but I know I'm about to find out the real reason, and I know it's going to fucking suck.

Call it premonition or foreshadowing, I know in

my bones that when I step out of this car, everything is going to change and there is no stopping it.

"Are you ready?" Kincaid asks, his hands straining the leather-covered steering wheel in a tight squeeze.

"No," I whisper. "But I don't think that matters, does it?"

The moment I step out of the car, I sense a difference in the atmosphere. The air seems denser, as though we're wading through it.

It makes breathing a chore. It makes my body feel heavier than it did a few moments before. Like gravity is stronger here, or like maybe my legs have been filled with sand.

Kincaid draws the staff from the back seat, careful this time to keep it wrapped tightly. He re-ties the thin ropes to secure the silver-threaded blanket in place. When he catches sight of me, his expression darkens. The corners of his mouth draw down into a grim frown.

He comes to me and gently pulls my arm through his. I don't stop him. I haven't the energy.

I know that without his help, I might not be able to walk, and if I can't walk, then I can't do what he wants of me. My end of the bargain will not be upheld. I shudder to think what he could do to me, or to Artemis, if I fail.

Holding onto Kincaid does make moving easier. Together, we take slow steps toward the gates of Belle-fontaine cemetery. When Kincaid releases me to open them, I nearly fall to my knees, unaware of just how much strength he'd been lending me.

"Why do I feel like this?" I ask, my voice a hoarse croak. Suddenly, my lips and mouth feel painfully dry, and when I try to swallow, it's like trying to force water through a dam.

I've felt something like it before. In the dead room and again at the morgue. But if I thought those times were bad, they have *nothing* on this. My stomach roils with acid, and I suck in cool night air to try to center myself.

Kincaid takes my arm once more and pats my hand. "It's spirit energy," he tells me.

"Can you feel it, too?"

Kincaid tilts his head down to me, and I roll my heavy head to the side to see him looking down on me with those otherworldly eyes. "No," he whispers. "I cannot."

Each step we take further along the path through the headstones is another brick added to my shoulders. Another book on my chest, pressing down.

We pass tall pillar-like headstones that look like knives jutting up from the earth in the moonlight.

Smaller, rounded headstones cower in the deepened shadows beneath wide-reaching oak trees. Farther in, crumbling mausoleums, statues, and older headstones crouch under the sky. Some broken, and others bent from age and decay.

"What does that mean? Why can I feel them?"

Kincaid's Adam's apple bobs and he squeezes my hand in an uncharacteristically reassuring gesture. "That's what we're here to find out."

I fall silent, the pressure on my lungs is too much to attempt speaking now.

A rushing sound fills my ears, like crashing waves. Rising and falling. Rising and falling.

They're whispers, I realize.

Like the whispers from the staff, but these are weaker. Even more distant. They are background noise. An annoying hum that I can't shake.

It doesn't take a genius to realize what they are. If I wasn't sure before. I am now.

They are spirits. The spirits of the dead people buried six feet below all around us.

"I can...hear...them," I say breathlessly.

When Kincaid tries to draw me further into the heart of the cemetery, I pull back, disentangling my arm from his. Gravity claims me the moment I do, and I fall hard onto my knees. My arms shake from trying to hold up the weight of my torso.

"*Na'vazēm,*" he calls, and I feel soft fingers brush against my shoulders, but my eyes are squeezed shut.

193

ELENA LAWSON

I lift one leaden hand and wave him off. "Can't… go…further."

"All right, *Na'vazēm*. No further."

I hear the *shhh* of rope tugging against fabric and moan. I knew he didn't bring the staff here for nothing, but I'm not ready. I'm not sure I can handle him unwrapping that devil stick right now.

I'm already stretched too thin. Pressed too small.

"There's something I need you to do for me, *Na'vazēm*."

Hot tears burn at the corners of my eyes.

I don't want to do this.

Please don't make me do this.

"In a moment, I am going to unwrap the Soul Scepter, and I am going to need you to take hold of it."

My eyes snap open, and I stare at him with unrestrained terror. I try to ask him if he's fucking insane, but I can't get enough air to voice my outrage.

"I know," he says, as though he's reading my thoughts. "I know it hurts, but if I'm right, this could take that pain away and replace it with something far more potent."

Grudgingly, I nod.

I just want this to be over.

Kincaid returns my nod and then finishes unraveling the scepter.

When he does, the pressure in the atmosphere intensifies. He's saying something to me, but I can't hear him over the barrage of angry whispers.

I cry out when Kincaid lifts me to my feet. Something wet trickles down my face, dripping from my chin. I taste copper and salted earth. I can't see through the tears.

Kincaid pries my stiff fingers apart and presses the smooth bar of the staff into my palm. As though of their own accord, as if magnetized, my fingers grip it.

A shockwave like that of an atomic bomb blasts out from within me. Vaguely, I realize Kincaid has been knocked back from the force of it. Trees sigh and crack. The earth beneath my feet rumbles and groans. Hair whips around my face, battering against my cheeks and sticking to the blood on my chin.

Finally able to breathe, I scream.

I scream long and loud as a sensation like cold lightning snakes through my body, electrifying my bones and boiling in my blood.

The earth no longer has a stronger pull on me. The weight on my chest is gone, replaced with an energizing lightness that makes me want to cry at its beauty. I've never felt anything like it.

It feels like…freedom.

It feels like…*power*.

The whispers have gone quiet. They are still there, but no longer overpowering.

"Paige!" I hear Kincaid shout and turn to find him watching me from a safe distance. I don't know what he sees, but his eyes are wide. His lips are parted as though he wants to speak but isn't sure what to say.

Ignoring him, I glance around, seeing the world as though through fresh eyes. Like a monarch surveying her kingdom. A whisper rises above the rest, and on instinct, I call it toward myself. It's as easy as breathing.

Once called by sheer force of my will, the whispering voice becomes clear.

"My brother did this," it says. "And he got away with it."

A phantom pain stabs into my chest, and I shove the voice back into the dark, trading it for another.

"I just wanted to hold my granddaughter before I went," an elder woman's voice croaks. "It's all I wanted…"

My heart twists, and I shove her back, too.

At the edges of my vision, shapes begin to form in the dark corners of the cemetery. Wisp-like black forms. Like living shadows detaching themselves from the whole.

A third voice vies for my attention, this one dull and muted even when I attempt to draw it near. It *feels* different than the others.

Making it out is a challenge. Continuing to operate on instinct, I pull from the power of the scepter, gritting my teeth.

"Asmodeus!" the voice booms, a deep throaty bellow that makes me search my immediate surroundings as though I'll be able to see the speaker.

Confused, I call to it. "Who are you?"

"You can hear me?"

The press of his spirit makes me tremble, and I begin to push him back, not wanting to talk to dead people anymore. I've done what Kincaid asked.

I want to go home.

But even as I think it, my body betrays me. Though I want to leave, I also don't want to let go of this staff.

The runes carved into the side of the base glow a shimmering gold.

"That's impossible," the voice roars.

I chuff out a laugh at that.

"It damn well should be," I mutter to myself.

"You *can* hear me."

"No shit," I retort, trying to do what I did before when I pushed the other spirits back, but this one is stubborn. He doesn't fade like the others.

"Wait!" he cries.

Something in his plea gives me pause.

"My name is Malphas," he rushes to say. "If you can hear me, I need you to tell Asmodeus I am dead. I've been trying to reach him. To reach anyone from this dark plane."

A shape wavers and snaps like a flag in the wind before me. The outline of a tall figure with broad shoulders and a wide chin. His features are a blur, but slowly, they too begin to materialize.

"Why should I do that?" I ask the shadow man, fear zapping my heart into a faltering rhythm.

"Who are you talking to?" Kincaid demands, the wonder now gone from his voice.

The ground beneath my feet trembles again, and I throw out an arm to steady myself, my nose bleeding anew.

"*Na'vazēm*, let go of the scepter," Kincaid calls from my left, getting closer now.

"Because," says the shadow man, whose eyes are now visible in the wavering shape of his face. Ruby red and unmoving. "If you don't, Asmodeus will die."

My jaw clenches at his words.

"Let go of the staff!" Kincaid growls through the rush of wind swirling around me. The earth still trembles, like something is slithering just beneath the surface of its crust. Like something ancient coming to life.

"What do you mean, he'll die?" I demand, loathing how the spirit man's promise makes my blood chill and something squeeze in my chest.

He stares, unblinking, and I know he doesn't intend to give me details, not without my doing as he's asked.

I growl to myself, trying to make a snap decision because I think Kincaid is right. I think I need to let go of this scepter. I don't know what will happen if I don't, and I'm not sure I want to find out.

If I say nothing and the shadow man is right and Kincaid dies, then I'll be free of him.

If I say nothing and Kincaid dies, I may also be giving up my only guaranteed way home.

"Damnit," I curse and turn to Kincaid, who is pushed back from me by some unseen force. He fights against it, trying to push forward, closer to me, without success. His booted feet slide backward in the earth every time he gains a yard.

"Kincaid," I call. "Malphas is dead."

He goes ghost-white, and for a heartbeat, I have to wonder if I've somehow just struck him dead. Kincaid looks between where I stand and the air around me, as though he too can sense the spirit of the man called Malphas.

"That isn't possible," he replies. "Now *let go* of the scepter."

I shrug at Malphas. "Sorry," I say. "I tried."

"No!" he roars, pressing forward. "Tell him...tell him *the sun sets in the east*."

I raise a brow at the shadow, wondering if I should tell him he's wrong. Instead, I turn back to a disheveled Kincaid. "He says 'the sun sets in the east.'"

Kincaid stops trying to advance and stares incredulously at me.

"Malphas?"

"It's me, brother," Malphas replies.

I choke on the blood still streaming from my nose and bend to spit it onto the earth. The instant I do, a resounding *boom* and *hiss* sounds around us.

Next to me, a headstone upturns, and I watch in muted horror as an emaciated hand reaches out from the dirt. All bone and dark, desiccated scraps of flesh and sinew. A stench like fresh rot makes my nostrils flare and my stomach turn.

"Kincaid!" I call, stumbling away from the thing trying to free itself from its grave. I nearly trip on another tombstone and whirl to find the curve of a skeletal head pushing up out of the ground, its hollow eyes searching. Its mouth unhinged but moving as though trying to speak without a tongue or lips.

I scream and something slams into my side. The scepter is knocked from my grasp, and the suffocating pressure slams back down on me, its weight magnified.

"Hold on," a familiar voice shouts through the din of heated whispers. I am lifted, and I feel the press of warm skin against my cheek as strong arms bear me away from the cemetery. Further and further until I can breathe again.

A car door opens, and Kincaid slides me into the passenger seat. I slump against it, feeling my eyelids begin to droop.

"Stay awake, *Na'vazēm*. I'll be right back."

When I turn my gaze to him, another scream attempts to liberate itself from my throat, but I don't have the energy to evict it.

Curved silver horns jut out from the sides of Kincaid's head. His black hair seems *light* compared to the color-absorbing pitch of his skin. His clothes, torn and in tatters, hang from his muscled demon form. A tail flicks out from behind him as he takes in my face, a look of pain twisting his features before he shoves the door closed and sprints inhumanly fast back the way we came.

22

I struggle to maintain consciousness, not wanting to be prone with all the spirits, reanimated corpses, and the demon who is going to be back any second hanging around.

This is not the time to succumb to my own weakness, but it seems my aching body and weary mind beg to disagree.

I'm close to losing my grip when the driver's side door creaks open and Kincaid slides into the seat. I do my best to twist myself into a position to face him. I don't want him at my back, especially not when he's all horned and demony.

I breathe a soft sigh of relief when I find he's no longer the demonic beast that carried me back to the car. He's Kincaid again. Wicked sneer and all.

"Can you still hear Malphas?" he demands.

I groan.

He shakes me a little until my eyelids peel back enough for me to meet his gaze. "Paige," he urges. "*Can you hear him?*"

I shake my head, but the gesture is so minuscule I'm not sure he's even seen it. I assume he must have because he leaves me be, releasing my arm in favor of the steering wheel. He thrusts the key into the ignition and the engine growls back to life.

"Something isn't right," he hisses, peeling out onto the road fast enough that I feel a little flutter in my belly. Kincaid slams his palms against the wheel and curses in a language I do not understand.

"Could you see him?" he asks as he pulls the wheel, making the car fishtail around a bend in the road. "Can you tell me what he looked like? I have to be certain."

I give my head a tiny shake again. "I could only see...his shape," I stammer, breathless. "Tall. Thick shoulders. Red, *red* eyes."

His knuckles go white with his grip on the wheel.

He doesn't speak for five long seconds, then he reaches his hand to me and gently presses the back of it against my forehead. His touch feels icy cold.

"You're burning up," he says, recoiling. "I'll see you home safe, *Na'vazēm,* but then there's somewhere I must go."

I cough weakly, trying to rid the blockage in my throat. "Where?"

I'm gripped with cold terror, and I can't say why, but I know that I don't want him to leave. As frightening as Kincaid is, he is also the only thing keeping me safe. Keeping me alive.

Startling myself with the thought, I realize that whether I want it or not, Kincaid is my one and only ally in Elisium. He is the only being who cares at all whether I live or die. Whether that's because he's a devilish bastard who has a morbid desire to find out what I am or not, he's all I've got until I can leave this place.

"Kincaid," I probe, my voice barely above a whisper. I can feel myself slipping away faster now. I dig my fingernails into the flesh of my wrist until I gain some more clarity. "*Where?*"

His yellow eyes flash in the light of a passing street-lamp, making them shine with malice. "To Hell," he mutters.

We make it back to the house in record time, and the moment the car comes to a jarring stop, my door is open, and Kincaid is there, lifting me out. I don't fight him, not even when he cradles me to his chest for a second time tonight. Instead, I let myself meld to his form. Beneath the tatters of his shirt, he is back to his normal self, and it's hard not to notice the difference between being carried by his monster, and being carried by him.

His smell, so strong this close up, tickles my nose with its alien scent. His warmth makes the sting of the cold, early-morning air on my skin bearable, and I try to cling to him more tightly.

"What happened?" I hear Artemis shout just after a door bangs open and Kincaid and I pass over the threshold. He sets me down gingerly on the bottom step in the foyer, and I lean into the banister, using the carefully carved wooden posts to support my weight.

The chiming of a bell precedes the approach of Kincaid's cat. It meows plaintively at me, coming to rest on the step above my head before it decides better of that and hops right onto my lap, nudging me with tiny clawed paws as though to wake me.

"She's depleted," Kincaid replies, and I note how his voice has changed, morphed into something oddly monotone. "Can you help her?"

Artemis lifts my hand from the step, ignoring a hiss from the cat, and tucks it between both of his. Unlike Kincaid, Artemis feels warm, and when my eyes flutter open again after a second, I'm startled at what I find.

That strange, eerie golden aura around Artemis is back again, pulsing brighter now than it had been before. His eyes shine as though tiny flashlights are fixed behind them.

It hurts to look at him, so I blink hard and turn my focus back to Kincaid.

"Yes," Artemis says. "I think so."

"Do it," Kincaid hisses, throwing a hand through his sweat-slicked black locks. He rushes to the small container in the corner by the door, the one with all the umbrellas and canes. He draws one out. It's taller than the others, more a short staff than a cane. Or perhaps a walking stick. It's black with shades of blue and emerald shimmering within and hooked near the top.

"I'll be back as soon as I can. Do not leave this house."

He taps the staff twice on the marble floor. Two sharp knocks echo through the foyer before Kincaid explodes into a plume of fire-flecked smoke and disappears.

There's a tense silence where neither Artemis nor I say a word. Then, unable to help it, a rumbling laugh erupts from my belly.

It aches in my sides and makes tears well in my eyes.

The cat is scared away and jumps from my lap to put distance between us.

"Um, *Paige?*" Artemis asks, and I realize the warm itch in my palm, running up my arm, is him healing me. It feels foreign and welcome all at once, and that, for whatever reason, only makes me laugh harder.

"Did you see that?" I ask, breathless, my energy returning with Artemis' help. I wave a half-limp arm toward where Kincaid was just a second before, hunching over from a smarting pain in my side.

An image of Dorothy clicking her glittery red shoes together while saying 'I wish I were home' comes unbidden to my mind.

I can't handle the hilarity of the comparison between Kincaid and sweet little pig-tailed Dorothy. I know it's ridiculous, but I can't stop laughing. I'm distantly aware that there's something fundamentally wrong with that, but it only adds to the hilarity.

Maybe this is it. Maybe I've finally lost my mind.

It's long overdue.

"Where did he go?" Artemis asks, ignoring the last of my barking laughs with only a raised brow in my direction.

I wipe a tear from my eye and shrug. "Off to see the wizard," I joke, making the laughter start up again. "The wonderful wizard of Oz."

Artemis grabs my hand more tightly to help me up. I nearly stumble, but catch myself on the banister, bent over and giggling like a child. "Okay, crazypants," he says. "Let's get you to bed."

KINCAID HAS BEEN GONE FOR A FULL NIGHT AND DAY. I thought I'd have to field an escape attempt from Artemis by now, but he's done the complete opposite of planning his departure.

He's ransacked the pantry and made himself comfortable in his new borrowed room, surrounded in expired crackers and canned soup. He's showered twice today, and had a several hour nap in the afternoon.

I wish I could sleep.

Other than the few hours where my body literally

shut down after Artemis got me into bed and cleaned the blood away from my face, I haven't slept a wink.

I lazily stroke Kincaid's cat's fur, pausing to scratch him behind the ears how he likes. His rumbling purr calms me enough that I can continue reading the leather-bound books I have set into two towers next to the high-backed chair in the library.

I've managed to start a fire on my own, which I'm pretty proud of. I even have a hot mug of long-expired tea that doesn't taste half bad sitting on the little table I dragged in from the next room.

The books did not disappoint. Some seemed to be ledgers of some kind, but a great many more are filled with all kinds of demon-privileged information. I doubt even mortals in command on the other side of The Hinge know half this stuff.

Of course, more than half the books in the library I cannot read at all, which I'm sure is why Kincaid agreed to allow me access to them. Those volumes are in a language I can't even identify, let alone understand.

I'm just about through a book that is basically an encyclopedia of daemonica and lists the names and traits of at least fifty different breeds of demon, when something in the air shifts and the scent of sulfur tickles my nose.

Shutting the book, I gently lift the cat and set him on the ground. He swats at me when I do, and I give him a look that says not to mess with me or he won't get any more pats.

"Kincaid?" I call, keeping my voice fairly low. It's nearing midnight if the clock on the wall can be trusted and Artemis said goodnight well over an hour ago. I don't want to wake him. Something tells me he still has some catching up to do with his sleep.

I'm about to go investigate when I hear his light footsteps approaching. Strange, but I've already grown accustomed to the sound of them. For a brief second, I consider taking up the fire poker as a weapon in case I'm wrong and it isn't him, but then he appears in the doorway and I relax, if only a little.

Dark circles claim the skin around his eyes, and his clothes, still in tatters, look to now be singed as well. He looks...

I can't think of the word right away, but then it dawns on me and something in my chest pangs.

He looks sad.

Terribly, *painfully*, sad.

That's when I remember how Malphas called Kincaid his brother. Whether by birth or choice, clearly learning of his death has hurt the demon before me.

It's an emotion Kincaid hasn't shown me before, and I don't like how my own belly yawns open with a pit of despair, forcing an empathetic response.

"*Na'vazēm*, what are you doing awake? It's late."

His tone is faraway. His gaze sweeps the carpet, never landing on any one thing.

I gulp, unsure of what to do with my hands and

wishing he would stop looking like a man going to his doom. "I—I couldn't sleep."

I tuck a strand of hair behind my ear and approach him cautiously. "What happened, Kincaid?"

His gaze flicks up for an instant at the use of his name, a curious gleam in his eyes that sputters out too quickly. "Hmm?"

"What happened?" I prod again, working to keep my tone level.

I'd been starting to wonder if he would return at all, and if he didn't, where that would leave me.

Where that would leave Artemis.

I can't help feeling glad he's returned from the bowels of Hell in one piece. "Why did you go?"

"I had to find out for myself if it was true," he replies in a whisper-soft voice.

"About Malphas."

He gives a tight nod.

"And?"

When Kincaid looks up again, a terrible tremor skitters down the length of my spine. His eyes are hard. His jaw is set.

"He's gone," Kincaid says. "Without a trace."

He sighs and bows his head. "Malphas is dead."

My hand lifts from my side, and I'm not sure what I was about to do, but I lower it again, cursing the desire to comfort him. Monsters don't need comforting.

Demons don't cry.

Kincaid breathes in deeply and his shoulders roll

back. His brows lower as he surveys my piles of books and the fire burning low in the hearth.

"I see you're making good use of your end of the bargain," he says, and for some reason, the words sting.

Kincaid brushes past me to flip through the top few volumes on the twin stacks of books and then sets them back down and goes to the shelves.

He brushes his long fingers over several titles, before pulling one out from the second to top shelf—one I couldn't have reached on my own—and splays it open between his hands.

I'm afforded an unobstructed view of his back through the tatters of his shirt. Two large horizontal tears in the fabric reveal a smooth and densely corded torso, but also...

Scars.

Two near identical scars mar the otherwise perfect masterpiece of his body. The large crescent-shaped burn scars mottle the flesh along the inner ridges of his shoulder blades.

He turns before I can get a better look, and I snap my gaze back to his face, not wanting him to know I was staring. Kincaid comes to me with the heavy book still spread between his hands.

"Here," he says tonelessly. "This is what you should be reading."

I take the proffered book, twitching when our fingers brush beneath its spine.

"But...it's a book on necromancy?"

Looking at the words on the page, I can see it's a handwritten text, as many of them are. In one hand there are small passages around a skeletal drawing in English. And in another hand, there are small bits of what I assume are someone's notes in a language I assume to be demonic. At the top of the page, it clearly reads, *Necromancy.*

Kincaid only stares in reply.

My skin bristles. "Is that what I am then?" I ask, hating how my voice cracks on the last word. "A necromancer?"

Kincaid's placid expression does not change save for the tiny jump of a vein at his temple. "I've never seen anything like what you did last night, *Na'vazēm*...but this is the closest label I can come up with."

What the hell is that supposed to mean?

He must see my confusion, because he brushes a hand over the shadow of dark scruff on his jaw and says, "Not only is it near impossible to kill one of the seven lords of Hell..." he trails off, going to stand near the fire and stare into its warm glow.

"But demons...we don't have souls, Paige. Diablim, *yes*. But not demons. You shouldn't have been able to commune with Malphas' spirit. It doesn't make any sense."

I consider what he's saying even though it makes me sick to my stomach. "Is that why Artemis glows with light, and you don't?"

His spine stiffens at that, but he makes no move to turn his attention back to me. "Yes."

"Then why could I—"

"Can you hear him now?" Kincaid asks suddenly, whirling on me so quickly I drop the book from my hands. "Can you still hear Malphas?"

I flounder for a response. His sudden change in demeanor is disconcerting.

"No," I stammer. "No, I haven't heard anything at all since I woke up yesterday."

It's not exactly true. I did hear some strange whispers near the galley kitchen, but I've steered clear of the area since then and they seem to have gone.

Kincaid's face falls.

In a knee-jerk reaction, I place a hand on his shoulder, and he starts. "I'm sorry for your loss," I tell him because isn't that what you're supposed to say when someone dies?

Haunted yellow eyes consider me carefully in the dim lighting of the room. The flicker of firelight bathes him in a soft orange hue.

He opens his mouth to say something in reply, then closes it again and reaches up to take my hand from his shoulder. He holds it for a moment in his and then presses it against my own chest and releases it.

He nods once and turns to go.

"Kincaid, wait," I blurt. "Will you leave again?"

I need to know.

Being here, in Elisium, alone, with Artemis as my

responsibility has been the most stressful twenty-odd hours of being on this side of The Hinge, and that's saying something.

If someone came for us, I wouldn't be able to protect him.

If there's anything I've learned since Artemis arrived, it's that fear for my own safety is nothing in comparison to fearing for the safety of someone else who is in your charge.

"No, *Na'vazēm*. I won't be leaving you. I hardly want you out of my sight."

He seems to struggle with some decision, his shoulders rippling with muscle as his fists clench and unclench at his sides. "You will come to the Midnight Court with me on the next moon," he says with finality.

"I need to make an appearance there briefly, and I can't trust you will be safe here without me. Not anymore."

I'm about to give him a resounding *hell no* before I remember I can't. Not if I want to uphold my end of the bargain and get out of here.

If there's any remote possibility that I can leave Elisium, go back to the mortal side of the river, I have to take it. If not for myself, then for Artemis.

I brought him into this mess and now it's my job to get him out.

"As you wish," I snap, and stoop to snatch up the book from the floor before strolling from the room.

"So, are you and Mr. Kincaid, like, boning?" Artemis' questioning voice breaks my concentration for the millionth time, and I groan in frustration, flushing scarlet.

"*No*," I grit out. "We are *not* boning."

He gives me a one shoulder shrug. "It's a valid question."

"Can you just stop talking. I can't concentrate with you blathering nonstop."

He makes a wounded face and gasps, but then falls back into forced silence with a roll of his eyes. "Fine."

"Give me your hands," I demand, reaching over my crossed legs to him.

He does as he's told, slapping his palms down against mine with another audible sigh. "It isn't going to work…" I hear him grumble beneath his breath.

I shush him and clasp his hands, sealing my eyes shut to find my center.

The book Kincaid gave me in the library four days ago has a lot of valuable information about necromancy. It's not exactly a how-to guide, but I've always been good at reading between the lines.

Apparently, Kincaid was right about demons not having souls, at least, if this book is to be believed.

Except, I saw and heard Malphas in that graveyard, which means he must have something *like* a soul, right?

Artemis' soul is easy to sense, which is why he's unwillingly become my practice dummy. According to the book—if I am a necromancer like Kincaid thinks—I should be able to feel Artemis' soul.

Not just see the glow of its aura like a ghostly form around him, but actually feel it, and if I wanted to, I should also be able to suck it out and then deposit it back inside him.

Obviously, I'm not going to try that quite yet. I'd be happy to settle for actually finding and feeling the thing, but we've been trying off and on for the last two days with no success.

"Ugh," I moan, dropping his hands after a further five minutes of teeth-grinding. My brain feels about ready to explode. "You're right. I can't do it."

"So, can we have a snack now? I'm starved."

I roll my eyes at him and wave a hand toward the door. "Go," I tell him, pinching the bridge of my nose with my thumb and forefinger to try and rid my skull of the incessant aching. "I'm not hungry."

"Suit yourself," he chimes. "I'll just bring you a glass of water."

"Thanks," I mutter, and then, pointing to my forehead, I add, "Hey, do you mind? It's really killing me again."

Artemis kneels back down and clasps my head between his palms. A burst of shuddering warmth ripples down my spine and when he lets me go a second later, the pain has ebbed and the black spots in my vision are gone.

"What would I do without you?" I say in a whisper before yawning. Artemis' ability always makes me want to curl up and take a nap.

He laughs. "Your head would probably explode."

I don't think he's wrong.

Artemis opens the door to leave but pauses in the doorway and then bends to pick something up from the floor.

"Is it your birthday or something?"

My brows furrow. "No," I reply. "My birthday isn't for another month. What is it?"

Artemis turns back around, a large flat box clasped between his hands. It's crisp white with a golden ribbon around its middle that's tied into a lazy bow at the top.

When Artemis sets it onto my lap, he lifts the tiny

tag hidden beneath a curl of gold ribbon. "It says your name on it."

Sure enough, when Artemis angles the tag toward me, I can see it reads *Paige* in a flowing script.

My mouth goes dry and my face must be a dead giveaway because Artemis snickers and his blue eyes go bright with delight. "You are such a liar. I knew you were boning him!"

I get up from the floor and give him a little shove, my skin itching with his accusation. "Stop saying that," I warn, but there's no mirth in the threat.

He narrows his eyes at me, a taunting smirk on the corner of his juvenile lips.

"Or you'll what?" he says, clearly trying to get a rise out of me. It's his favorite thing to do.

I don't know why I thought having a pubescent teen around twenty-four-seven was a good idea.

Artemis may have seen some shit in his short life, but he's still a kid. And I'm starting to find that the more comfortable he gets, the more annoying he becomes.

"Or," I start, stammering in my indignant fury, "or I'll make Kincaid return you to those awful Diablim women."

He grins triumphantly, "Because you have that demon *whipped*."

"Oh my god. Get out." I growl. "Go get your damned snack before I make good on that promise."

Artemis laughs all the way out the door and down the hall. We both know I would never send him away.

I wait to make sure he's really gone before I set the box down on the bed and tiptoe to the door. I shut it, silently turning the knob so it doesn't make any noise and then padding back to the bed.

I study the tag for a second time, my blood rushing in my ears. There's no one else in Elisium who knows I'm here except maybe that Tori girl and the Diablim from the demon market.

It has to be from Kincaid, but why?

We haven't spoken in four days. Not since I stormed out of the library with my book.

I haven't even seen him. He hasn't left the house as promised, but he also hasn't left his rooms. They're at the opposite end of the hall, past the stairs leading down to the front foyer. Artemis ran into him the other night. Said he was stumbling drunk and had his horns out.

A few times, I considered going to him. I had questions to ask and needed to request that he get more food before Artemis ate everything there was and we were back to starving again. But I didn't.

Each time, I came up with some excuse not to. Even last night, when I made it all the way to what I thought was his bedroom door, I still chickened out.

I heard a noise from inside and bolted, afraid he would come to the door still in his demon form.

And now it seems he is sending me gifts?

What am I supposed to make of that?

I finger the smooth satin ribbon and bite my lower lip, trying to think of a reason not to open it. I could just go and plop it down in front of his door with a scribbled *no thank-you* beneath my name on the tag. Except…I don't want to do that. My curiosity is piqued.

"Oh, just open it already."

I squeal like a stuck pig and whirl to find Artemis in the doorway munching an apple. "You know you want to."

I wonder how there isn't steam coming out of my ears. "You are infuriating, has anyone ever told you that?"

"More times than I can count."

"Not surprising." I huff and tear the ribbon from the box because Artemis is right. I *do* want to open it.

Next comes the lid, and I'm left staring at something that's carefully wrapped in white tissue paper. A note card is tucked between two folds at the middle. I tug it free and hold it up, determined to get this whole ordeal over with.

I know Artemis is going to read it anyway, so I read what it says aloud.

"

Midnight.

-K

"

"That's all it says?" Artemis says around a mouthful of apple as he comes to stand next to me and peer into the box. Some juice drips from his chin, and he rushes to wipe at it with the back of his sleeve.

I hand him the notecard as proof and peel back the tissue paper to reveal the contents of the box.

My mouth falls open.

"What is that?" Artemis asks, lifting up one tiny edge of the fine fabric.

I smack his apple juice-covered fingers away.

"Is it a dress?" he tries again.

With warring emotions of dread and wonder, I gently lift the dress from the box, mindful of the delicacy of the thing. It's unlike anything I've ever seen. Glittering black lace-like patterns stretch up from the waist like branches, curling and thickening to cover the area where my breasts would be. The sleeves are the thinnest gossamer.

The skirt is bunched clumps of the softest fabric I've ever touched. On closer inspection, I can see that it isn't just bunched fabric, but purposefully and artfully twisted sections to make it look like it's covered in black roses.

There's some boning in the top, and when I turn it to inspect the back, I can see there's a section of thin silk laces in gunmetal silver running from the shoulder-blades all the way down to the tailbone.

"It's not a dress. It's fucking artwork."

"Midnight, hey?" Artemis says thoughtfully, gobbling up what remains of the apple core and leaving only the stem. "Guess that means he wants you to wear it."

That's when I notice the dainty shoes hidden beneath the hem. The same gunmetal hue of the laces at the back of the dress.

"Is the full moon tonight?" I ask as if Artemis will know.

He shrugs. "Beats me."

I'd all but forgotten.

You will come to the Midnight Court with me on the next moon, Kincaid had said. I didn't realize that would be so soon.

I drop the dress back into the box and whirl on Artemis. "Tell me everything you know about the Midnight Court."

❧ 24 ❧

The Diablim woman called Pattywort tugs at my unruly hair, tutting as she combs out sections of it with a boar bristle brush.

I had to send Artemis away nearly twenty minutes ago because he was clearly having too much fun watching the woman poke and prod me into beauty.

She showed up around ten. A short, slender woman with pointed ears and even pointier teeth. Pattywort carried a large leather case and a foul attitude with her into my room, introducing herself as "the help Kincaid ordered."

Apparently, I could not be trusted to look my best for this event on my own.

"Do you *ever* brush these knots, girl?" Pattywort chastises, being none too gentle as she drags the bristles through section after section of my hair.

"I would if I had a brush," I grumble in reply. I've

been using my fingers to get the majority of the tangles out after washing each day, but with hair as thick as mine, it doesn't do much to help.

We fall back into silence as Pattywort tames my hair into submission, a sour expression on her face until finally, she pins the last piece away from my face and stands back to admire her handiwork, her bony fingers on her knobby hips.

"There," she declares in a great exhalation of air, her pointed teeth visible in her slight grin. "Even with the unfortunate color, I don't think it looks half bad."

I roll my eyes for the tenth time since she arrived. It's easier now that I know she isn't going to try to eat me with those teeth. She's wicked enough with her words that she needn't use them. And I doubt any Diablim would be stupid enough to harm Kincaid's property.

Pattywort checks a slender gold watch on her left wrist and pouts. "Doesn't leave us much time, now. Guess you'll be getting your wish after all, miss."

I grin triumphantly.

When I saw all the pots and tubes and creams in her case, I shuddered, wondering what exactly she would make me into using all those colors and brushes. I asked her to put as little of the stuff on me as she could without provoking Kincaid's wrath.

I was already property of a lord of Hell, but I'd be damned if I went anywhere looking like his pretty little doll.

"Don't look so pleased with yourself," Pattywort says, clucking her tongue as she draws out a pot of white moisturizer and sets to lightly brushing it over my face. "You're lucky to have such a lovely bone structure. I shan't need more than a little shading to get you looking your best."

"I've never worn makeup," I blurt, unsure what prompted me to say it, and immediately regret my choice.

Pattywort's brush stills for a moment on my face before she sets back to work.

"Hmm," she says with a pinch between her brows. "Then let's make an event of it, shall we?"

She tucks the pot and brush away and prods me to standing. She then spins me around and sits me back down, this time facing me away from the vanity's mirror.

I'd be lying if I said there isn't a little hum of excitement buzzing in my veins, making my belly feel light and fluttery. I've never cared much to have makeup— there wasn't any point when no one would ever see me wearing it save for Ford.

But, as I imagine most little girls do, I often wondered how I would look wearing it for the first time. I just never imagined that first time would be while being held captive in a demon's house across The Hinge in Elisium.

While a Diablim woman applied said makeup.

Because I was going to a Diablim event with a

demon.

Surreal doesn't even begin to describe it.

"Close your eyes," Pattywort demands, and I do. Light brush strokes flick over my eyelids. "Not much I can do about those eyes of yours," she muses. "If Kincaid had warned me, I could've brought some colored contacts for you to wear at the Court."

"What did Kincaid tell you, exactly?"

I peel back an eyelid to see her frowning. "Only that he would be bringing someone to the Court with him this eve and wanted her to blend in with the other courtiers."

Of course he would want me to blend in. He'd warned me once before of the dangers of standing out. It's why he didn't leave the house over the last four days. Not even once. He said he wouldn't be leaving me alone anymore. That it isn't safe.

It made the prospect of going to a place where—if Artemis is right—there will be Diablim as far as the eye can see more than a little daunting. And not just any Diablim, upper levels. The most powerful beings in all of Elisium. Apparently, even Nephilim are known to attend. With the occasional angel showing up to the festivities.

"How well do you know him?" I ask Pattywort.

"Who?"

"Kincaid."

Another frown.

"I don't think anyone knows him very well, dear,"

she says, and I sense a tension in the words. I don't miss how she's lowered her voice, and I bet if I opened my eyes, I'd see her beady black ones flitting toward the door.

Unperturbed, I press on. "Why not?"

Pattywort sighs. "Because that's how the lord likes it. He's never been one to flaunt his pomp and circumstance—like some of the other lords. Though he's been acting peculiar of late…"

Her tone's changed to one of intrigue and her voice has become hushed.

"He bought that healer boy out from under a few Diablim just last week. That makes two slaves he's purchased in barely two weeks when he's never purchased one before."

My back stiffens, and I hope she doesn't notice. No one knows why Kincaid bought me, save for the lord himself, and I don't think he would like anyone asking questions about it. In asking Pattywort about him, I could be putting her in danger of getting too curious. And in turn, in danger of meeting the business end of Kincaid's silvery horns.

"Right," I say, licking my lips, trying to put an end to the conversation.

But Pattywort isn't sated yet. She leans in, pausing in her brushing of some soft powder on my cheeks. "Curiouser still how he has you both here, living beneath his roof as though you're both guests instead of slaves…"

I open my eyes to see her black ones glimmering with intrigue. She's trying to glean information from me, I realize, and my fingers curl under the chair's edge, steadying me as I attempt to keep my face impassive.

"I don't pretend to know his intentions," I say. "I only do as he commands."

This reply seems to subdue Pattywort's curiosity, and she deflates a little, setting back to work with more vigorous strokes of her brush along the bottom edge of my cheekbones.

"Suppose I shouldn't be surprised," she says on a sigh. "The lord has always been a little *off*. I once saw him save a stray kitten from becoming sold off as dinner at the market, you know. Some might've thought he meant to eat the thing himself, but I know better," she says with the cavalier smirk of someone who thinks she's in the know.

"I saw how he coddled the thing to his chest, tucking it into the fold of his jacket against the wind and cold. He never meant to eat it. He meant to save it from *being eaten*."

It's clear Pattywort expects me to hold up my end of the conversation, so I swallow hard and ask, "Why would he do that? He's a demon. Why would he care about a stray cat being eaten?"

Surely, he'd done much worse things prior to his escape from Hell.

All the while, I'm wondering if that kitten he saved

is the nameless white cat with the belled collar who now lives in the house with him. I'm thinking it must be.

"A curious thing for a demon to do, no doubt," she says. "But darkness and light often hide in the most surprising of places."

"What does that mean?"

"Your Kincaid wasn't always as he is now, you know," she answers in a hush as she sweeps a wand of heartsblood crimson over my lips. "Once, he was an angel, and I think deep down a part of him still remembers that."

She says this as though it's something to be ashamed of, with a sneer curling her upper lip and the gleam of disgust in her beady eyes.

I can't help feeling the opposite.

Kincaid was an angel?

I can hardly picture it and am immediately wondering if this Diablim woman is blowing smoke. Or maybe if she's insane.

The beast I saw tear that daeva to shreds could not be anything other than what it looked like. A demon. There's no way those haunting yellow eyes could've ever belonged to anything else.

Pattywort startles me with two bony fingers gripping my chin. She jerks my gaze to meet hers. "But don't tell him I said so, or he'll have my head on a platter. Got it?"

I shake off her grip and pleat my fingers in my lap. "Yeah. Fine. I won't say anything."

"Good girl," Pattywort says with a little pat on the top of my head. She gives me a last once-over and a slow smile pulls her lips apart to reveal her pointed teeth again.

The more I see them, the less horrifying they become. In some strange way, they suit her.

"I think that'll about do it. Let's get you into the gown and then have a look, shall we?"

Pattywort leads me from the stool and away from the mirror to dress. I try to protest as she strips me down, but she bats my hands away, telling me I'd never be able to get the gown on by myself. Not with all the laces and fine, thin fabric.

"You'll shred it to ribbons tugging on it like that," she scolds. "Let go."

Giving up, I let her dress me as though I am the doll I didn't want to be after all, staring at a particularly large crack in the corner of the ceiling to distract myself.

"All right. We're done," Pattywort announces, checking her watch again with a little gasp. She shoves me in front of the mirror, her face turning a shade of blanched gray. "Hurry and have a look, miss. We don't want to keep Master Kincaid waiting."

What I find in the mirror is a version of myself I never would've thought existed.

I thought once Pattywort was through I wouldn't

look at all like myself, but I'm pleasantly surprised to find that I still do. The Diablim woman has worked some magic into my dull skin and ratty hair.

She's made the faded purple and pink dye look like it might have been a purposeful choice. She's pinned back two sections on either side of my face and placed a small headpiece atop my skull like a crown. It helps to hold my hair in place—she's wrapped sections of it around the thin silver circlet—and a tiny black jewel dangles against my forehead.

It makes me look somehow regal.

Like a dark queen.

My face is still my own, only more polished and refined. My skin glows with a radiance like it never has before and my silver eyes look extra bright from the wash of mascara and liner on my lashes. It all looks like it could be natural, save for the deep heartsblood color of my lips.

Though I am not the masterpiece. The dress steals the spotlight. Making me look curved and bowed in all the right places. My breasts were nothing to brag about, but with the reaching branches of lace cupping them, casting shadows on my skin through the wisp thin material, they look almost airbrushed.

Even I have to admit it—I look good.

Pattywort has crafted me into someone who looks worthy of such finery. I lift my chin, wishing I could feel like it were true.

"Come, miss. Let's not keep him waiting."

Kincaid is waiting by the front door, a scowl on his face, his hooked black staff clasped tightly in his grip.

I'm surprised to find I'm nervous when I catch sight of him in his fine clothes. His black hair is thrown back, only one small curl of it out of place, but it almost looks purposeful the way it bends over his brow.

He wears a tailored jacket much like the one he wore the day he purchased me from the demon market. It's long and detailed through the collar and cuffs. Beneath he wears a loose-fitted dress shirt tucked into trim dark trousers.

When he catches sight of me nearly stumbling down the stairs in the cursed heels he sent along with the dress, he stills.

His lips part and from the way he's staring I think

he's about to change his mind about the whole thing and make me stay here.

Pattywort clears her throat when we reach the bottom of the stairs. She drops the small train and bows before Kincaid. "I hope my work is to your liking, my lord?"

Kincaid nods. "Yes," he says, something scratching in his voice. "You may go. Thank you for your services."

Pattywort tosses me a wink before scuttling out the front door, sealing it behind her.

"How are—"

"I chose—"

We speak at the same time, and I drop my gaze, turning what I'm sure is a very unflattering shade of red. All the while cursing the riotous nerves wreaking havoc in my belly.

I want to think it's because of where Kincaid's taking me, but I worry it's for another reason entirely. I thought after four days spent apart, maybe the strange after-effects of his power over my desire would have waned. It seems I was mistaken.

My traitorous heart pounds wildly behind my rib cage as his hungry eyes rove over every inch of Patty-wort's handiwork.

"You go ahead," I say awkwardly, having entirely forgotten what I was even going to say to him anyway.

"I chose black, thinking it might help you blend in more easily," he says, and I startle when the press of two warm fingers lifts my chin so I have to hold his gaze again.

He looks over my face, settling his yellow eyes on mine. He snorts and releases me with a sigh. "I can see now that I was wrong."

I cock my head at him, unsure I catch his meaning. Or rather, hoping I'm wrong about it.

"You could never blend in, *Na'vazēm.*"

Is…is he saying I look beautiful?

"It's almost midnight," I croak, and the spell is broken.

Kincaid straightens and whatever trace of humanity I'd found in his gaze vanishes. "So it is," he says, his voice back to his usual dull monotone.

He holds out an arm to me.

"Take it," he orders when I hesitate. "I would keep you close tonight, *Na'vazēm. Very* close."

THE DRIVE TO THE MIDNIGHT COURT IS QUICK AND quiet. Kincaid stares out his window, and I can see his jaw working in the light thrown over him every so often from the streetlamps.

I wonder what he's thinking, but I'm too afraid to ask.

He asked me once more when we first got into the vehicle if I'd heard the voice of his fallen brother, Malphas, at all since we returned from Bellefontaine cemetery. When I told him I hadn't, but that I could

ELENA LAWSON

hear others sometimes, he fell into a stony silence and hasn't spoken again.

If he did, I think I know what he might say. What he might ask of me.

I've read enough of the necromancy book now to know that the staff he purchased from Tori—the Soul Scepter—is a thing that serves to enhance a necromancer's power.

It whispers because immortal souls are trapped within it.

It enhances a necromancer's power by harnessing energy from those imprisoned spirits.

I never want to touch it again, but I know it's only a matter of time before Kincaid will ask me to, and if I want to hold up my end of the bargain, then I must.

"Is that it?" I ask, pointing into the distance. The question is more to rid the air of this tepid silence than to get an answer.

Of course, it's the Midnight Court. The palace shines like a beacon in the dark. A Greco-Roman style building with a massive domed middle and smooth columns to either side, it shines with spotlights aimed up against its walls from the grassy lawn at its feet.

"Yes," Kincaid answers grimly as we pull into a queue leading to the entrance. There, fairy lights twinkle in the arched entryway. Diablim walk along a carpet that looks like it's a swath cut from the midnight sky, complete with a smattering of stars.

A line of horned men in tailored suits and white

gloves wait to take the keys of the guests and park their cars for them. *Valet*, my mind supplies.

Since we have our own driver, when it's our turn to pull up, Kincaid merely steps out, extending a hand to me from where he stands outside.

A sweet smell like lilac and honeysuckle tickles my nose, and the murmur of too many voices rises above the sound of a band playing from somewhere within the palace.

Faces twisted with hooked noses and bright red eyes turn to take me in as I step out of the gangstermo- bile and Kincaid tugs my arm through his.

Those whispers quell as Kincaid leads me past dallying guests and onto the carpeted runway leading inside.

"Try to relax," Kincaid says in a hush. "They can scent fear from a mile away."

My lungs seize, and I force myself to stand a little straighter—the boning in the top part of my dress helps me stay there—with my chin held high.

Kincaid is right of course. I am afraid, there's no denying it, but I also cannot deny my mounting curiosity as I take in all the new sights, smells, and sounds.

On Kincaid's arm, I am untouchable.

In his shadow, I am safe.

I don't have to be afraid.

There's something exhilarating about that. And as I

tilt my head to one side to take in his stoic, regal face, something clenches low in my belly.

Diablim incline their heads as we pass, making no secret of their own interest in the silver-eyed girl on his arm. I can't help noticing in furtive glances how some have that light in their eyes, like Artemis does. How they glow with different, brightly colored auras if I let my eyes go unfocused. A couple gleam brightly, but most don't shine at all, or very, *very* little.

We enter under a canopy of dark flowers and shining silvery thorns and Kincaid steers me down a smaller corridor than the one everyone else seems to be taking towards the sound of the music.

"Where are we going?" I ask in a hush as he pulls me more quickly around a bend and down a flight of stone stairs. I struggle to keep up, the small heels on the strappy shoes making the decline more difficult than I care to admit. I'm two seconds from falling flat on my face the entire time.

"Kincaid?"

It gets darker the further down we go. The scent of earth and something sharp like the tang of spilled whiskey tickles my nose.

"Kincaid," I repeat, more firmly this time, pulling at his hold on my arm.

We stop abruptly, and my arm is freed of his. Strong hands grip my waist and press me fast against the chilled stone at my back. Hickory and sandalwood envelop me as he presses in close.

I can feel the whisper of his breath against my lips.

It burns where his thumbs push into the sensitive skin at my waist, holding me tightly. His yellow eyes spark like flames in the shadows.

Panic and longing begin a dangerous dance beneath my breastbone. Whirling and bending. Breaking.

"What are you do—"

"I can feel your desire for me, *Na'vazēm*," he growls, and I can hear his teeth grind. *"It's driving me mad."*

I open my mouth to deny it. I want to blame him for why my body is aching with the desire for him to touch me more. To squeeze me tighter. But that would be a lie.

Even if how I feel is some fucked-up side-effect of Kincaid's power over desire, it would be a lie to say I don't like how it feels. That I don't crave it.

Crave him.

"Stop," he demands in a roar that echoes back from the stone walls around us. I don't realize I've placed my hands lightly on his chest until he jerks beneath my touch. His breaths come hard and heavy, and in the dark, I can see the tips of two silvery horns emerging beneath his black hair.

I look at his lips. Their fullness. The dip of his cupid's bow.

I've never been kissed, and I don't think I much cared about that fact until right now. My thighs squeeze and something flips low and hard in my belly.

An emotion that's one-part fear and two-parts frenzy grips me.

"*Paige*," he says on a breath, and I can't hold back anymore.

I want him to kiss me.

It's wrong, and I shouldn't want it, but there it is. The truth in all its great and terrible clarity.

I want this demon to kiss me.

As soon as I think it, he's there. A rough growl vibrating in his chest before his lips are against mine. They are hard and unyielding, stealing what little breath remains in my lungs. His fingers press almost painfully into my flesh and my fingers curl tightly into the collar of his jacket, pulling him closer. His body is hot where it touches me.

I let go of his jacket in favor of his shoulders, and his chest comes hard against mine, pressing into my breasts. His hips tuck in tightly between my thighs as he sweeps in with his tongue, drawing a stuttering moan from my chest.

His hands creep up from my hips, squeezing at my waist and then my ribs. Until one curls around the back of my neck, securing me to him. I surrender, marveling at the sensations making me dizzy and alert and confused all at once.

Something sings like electricity in my blood, and if Kincaid doesn't stop soon, I'm afraid I might come blissfully unraveled. Or that my heart will give out from trying to keep tempo with his.

Teeth scrape over my lower lip, and I whimper against Kincaid's mouth. My sex throbs like it has its own heartbeat as Kincaid presses his hardened length against me, and though it should be, it hardly feels softened between several layers of fabric.

He draws back, both of us breathless. I wonder if his head is spinning as violently as mine is.

"*Mea Na'vazēm*," he hisses and dips in to steal another rough kiss from my lips.

When he moves back a step and straightens his jacket, I nearly fall to the floor, but manage to brace myself on a notch in the stone wall. My legs feel like they're filled with air instead of blood and there are strange yellow spots dancing in my vision.

It takes me a full moment of shuddering breaths before I feel I can stand on my own two feet again. All the while my mind races to catch up to what my body just did. What it just allowed to happen.

What it just enjoyed.

Kincaid, a look of devilish amusement on his face, merely waits for me to be ready.

"We should get inside," he says, and once I've straightened back to my full height, he extends his hand to me.

I right my silver circlet and press my palms down against the bodice of the dress, trying to smooth out any evidence of the crimes I just committed in it. Then I take Kincaid's hand.

He tugs me into his chest and wraps an arm around

my back. My stomach drops to my toes at his penetrating stare.

"We've only just got here," he says, his burning gaze dipping low to the curve of my neck and lower still to my chest pressed against his. There's a strain in his voice when he speaks again. "But I already want to leave."

My breath catches.

"Then let's hurry," I say, shocking myself with how bold the words sound coming from my lips. I rub the tip of my index finger over the corner of Kincaid's mouth, erasing a tiny crimson smear there.

He stares at me curiously. Obviously, I've shocked him, too.

Raising a brow, he regards me with a predator's interest, making my toes curl.

"Yes. Let's."

❧ 26 ❧

We don't go back the way we came. Kincaid guides me further below ground instead, through a labyrinth of stone corridors until I begin to hear a cacophony of sound. Dinging and chiming and a sound like the scrolling numbers of a flip clock.

Cheers and clanging and incessant ringing.

I don't put two and two together until Kincaid tugs me through a coded door and onto a gambling floor. Lights flash and devilish faces grin and grimace. It seems to go on as far as I can see.

Slot machines and table games and small circular bars spilling foamy beer into tall glass mugs. A thrill goes through me at the sight. It's just how I imagined a casino would be in real life, except the patrons here are not mortal men and women in various states of wealth.

They are Diablim.

Charred faced and red-eyed. Winged and tailed. Some notice us as Kincaid leads me through the throng. The ones that do bow to their lord. Some try to shout greetings to him over the din, though their words are swallowed up by bells and shouts from across the room.

The cavernous space makes all the sounds echo back, amplifying them. A drunk salamander nearly spills his drink on me as we pass, but Kincaid deftly twirls me out of the way, knocking the man's beverage from his clumsy fingers with a glare.

The Diablim cowers when recognition flares in his droopy eyes.

Then, tucked more closely to his side, Kincaid rushes me out a hidden door behind a bank of slot machines and into another stairwell.

When the heavy door clicks shut behind us, it's like all the noise we left behind has been suctioned up by a vacuum. Only a muffled version of it remains. Like I'm hearing it through wads of cotton stuffed into my ears.

"What was that place?"

Kincaid smirks. "My casino," he replies. "Have you never been to one before?"

He seems to realize his mistake only a second after the words leave his lips and they press into a taut line. "Right," he says, his tone a dangerous whisper. "I suppose you haven't."

I brush a hand over his jaw, trying to erase the frown turning down the corner of his mouth. "I have now," I tell him with my best replica of a smile.

He doesn't buy it.

Kincaid removes my hand from his face, but doesn't let it go, instead squeezing it lightly between his long fingers. "Fifteen minutes," he promises. "We'll just stay for fifteen minutes and then we can go, all right?"

I chew my lower lip.

I *do* want to leave, but I also want to stay.

"What is it, *Na'vazēm?*"

Shaking my head, I lift my gaze back to his. It isn't important, and frankly, I don't know how I would explain it to him anyway. Instead of trying, I ask a question that I've wanted an answer to for weeks.

"What does that mean?"

"What does what mean?"

"*Na'vazēm,*" I do my best not to butcher it this time.

Kincaid's brows draw ever so slightly together, and I worry it means something awful.

"It means..." Kincaid says and licks his lips. A slight squint in his faraway gaze tells me he's struggling to explain something.

"The pronunciation isn't perfect, but it means something like...*lost girl.*"

I cock my head at him.

"Oh."

"Oh?"

I shrug. "I thought it might've been something…*offensive.*"

In a way, I suppose it is, but it's also the truth.

I was—and in a lot of ways, I still am—a lost girl. A girl with a lost childhood. A girl with a lost heritage. A girl who didn't even know she wasn't just a girl.

Kincaid chuckles, and the hearty sound lifts my lips into a real smile. Then he shakes his head like I've said the most ridiculous thing he's ever heard, and we begin to walk again, up the stairs and toward the music.

As we near the full moon festivities, Kincaid's tension grows. The ease of a few moments ago is replaced with rigidity. His mask is fully back in place by the time we come to a heavy velvet curtain and stop.

On the other side, I can hear the music dip and swell to the clatter of heels dancing on a marble floor. It's so different from the scene found deep in the earth below their feet. It's elegance versus vulgarity.

"Do not leave my sight," Kincaid says without turning and then sweeps the curtain away and pulls me through.

The glow of suffused yellowish light dapples the grand ballroom. A band is tucked into one corner of the room and banquet tables laden with foreign foods line the walls. Hooked nosed waiters pass through twirling couples and laughing Diablim to hand out golden goblets whose contents seem to sizzle and steam.

The whole place smells of lilac, honeysuckle, and something reminiscent of fire smoke.

I'm gaping and I know it, but I can't seem to lift my jaw back up off the floor. If it weren't for the horns and tails and intermittent leathery wings, I could almost pretend this was some kind of fairytale.

A grand ball like the masquerade in Labyrinth, except these aren't masks. They are real faces, sporting real teeth. And if I'm not careful, those teeth could bite.

One by one, heads turn in our direction. They incline to their lord. I study a whorl of black in the white marble at my feet, so I don't lose my nerve.

The music slows and then drops, taking my stomach with it.

Kincaid leans into my side. "Dance with me," he says. Not a question, but also not quite a demand.

"If it'll make them stop staring," I whisper harshly back, letting him lead me out onto the floor.

"It won't."

He takes my waist and puts his body into a perfect dancer's form. That's when I remember something I wish I'd thought of three seconds ago.

"Wait," I stammer as the music rises again. "I can't dance."

"Anyone can dance, *Na'vazēm*. Follow my movements and feel the music."

He begins to move, stepping forward and then back, tilting gently to one side as the song of a violin rises and then parrying to the right and spinning as a second joins the first.

"Eyes to me," Kincaid whispers as other dancers crowd around us, all of them dancing the same way as their lord.

"To me," he repeats, and I gulp, bringing my gaze up to meet his. There's a wild fluttering in my belly, and I feel like if I'm not watching my feet, they're going to step all over him.

"Shall I make it easier for you?" he asks with a wicked tilt to his eyes.

I'm not sure what he means, but I nod, not wanting to make a total fool of myself in a room full of demons. I already have their attention; I don't need their scorn.

Kincaid uses his power to dip inside of me. The press of his ability makes my body loose and malleable as clay. The whisper of his phantom touch sends shivers all over my body as he spins me effortlessly through the gathered courtiers.

Without my fear or inhibition, moving with him is as easy as breathing, and I revel in the feel of it. Of him.

When the song finally ends and we come to a stop, Kincaid releases his hold on me and leans down to press his lips to my ear. "See," he says. "Anyone can dance."

"Hey, stranger," someone says, and I feel the brush of a shoulder against mine.

I blink into the vivid violet hue of Tori's eyes. She

squints at Kincaid with her hands on her hips. "Thought you weren't going to bring your friend?"

Tori looks resplendent in a sheath of a dress that is so light a shade of lilac that it could be mistaken for silver. The yellowish cast of the light in the room makes her skin seem less ashen than it did under the dull lighting in her shop. Her face shines with the addition of a fine gold powder brushed over her cheekbones and in the corners of her eyes.

"You're beautiful," I blurt before I can stop myself. As if she didn't already look gorgeous enough, she has a faint lavender glow around her and a light beneath her already vivid eyes.

Her soul shines just as much as she does.

She regards me with a crooked brow. "Thanks," she says with an awkward smirk. "But I don't think anyone here tonight can hold a candle to what you've got going on here."

Tori makes a vague gesture at my dress and flickers her hand over my face. "I mean. What even *is* that material? It looks like spider silk."

My face warms.

"Anyway, I'm glad you came," she continues, completely cutting off something Kincaid was about to say and earning herself a scathing look. "You two are going to be the talk of Elisium for, like, *ever*."

"Tori," Kincaid grumbles. "Is there something you want?"

"Oh," she says, a hand to her chest in mock insult.

"Have I insulted you, oh great and powerful one? You're the one who showed up with a date for, oh I don't know, the first time ever. People are taking bets on how long it will be before you eat her."

A small sound squeaks past my lips at that.

Kincaid wraps an arm loosely around my shoulders. "And what's the general consensus?"

"A week," Tori says with a shrug.

Kincaid tips his head this way and that as though he might agree with that assumption.

I elbow him in the ribs, and he turns a haughty glare in my direction. I would cower, but there's no real ire in it. In fact, he seems almost too pleased with himself. The bastard.

"Oh, by the way, Dantalion is here. He popped in right after everyone started whispering about the great lord Asmodeus not arriving solo to the party."

Kincaid's face pinches. "Where is he?"

Tori glances around. "Not sure, but I saw him just before you came in."

"I'm sorry, who is Dantalion exactly?"

Tori looks at me like I might be dull. She jabs a thumb at me and raises a brow at Kincaid. "She serious?"

But Kincaid is too busy scanning the guests in attendance to bother answering her.

She regards me with a curious sort of pity. "He's one of the other lords," she says as though it were the most obvious thing in the world.

"Oh," I say, suddenly wary and trying to see if I can spot him in the crowd.

Tori snags two goblets from a tray as a waiter passes and hands me one.

"You need to get out more," she says and takes a long sip of the fizzing drink.

It smells of sugared plums and something rotten. I must make a face because Tori says, "It doesn't taste how it smells. Trust me. Try it."

"There's my brother," a deep voice slithers into our conversation.

Kincaid stiffens as a man in a deep cherry jacket with golden stitching in flower shapes—that somehow also manage to look like screaming faces—pats him on the back.

Dantalion's grin shows off two rows of perfect white teeth set into a square jaw. His eyes are like sapphires, and his hair is a halo of gold.

"Dantalion," Kincaid says gruffly by way of greeting, eyeing his brother suspiciously. I don't miss how he steps to one side, angling his body to conceal me in such a way as not to be noticed.

It doesn't work.

Dantalion's deep ocean eyes alight on me and spark with a keen interest. His smile returns with a renewed vigor. "Brother," he says in a chastising tone. "You're being rude. Won't you introduce me to your exquisite companion?"

Kincaid's right fist clenches tightly at his side, and

for a brief moment, I think he might strike Dantalion. I stay his hand with a light brush of my fingertips over the strained white of his knuckles and step out from behind him.

"My name is Paige," I say, inclining my head like I've seen the others do when Kincaid passes. "It's nice to meet you."

Dantalion, eyes alight, steps in close to snatch my free hand and presses his lips to the back of my palm. His fingers caress the sensitive flesh on the inside of my wrist, provoking a shudder from my bones.

"The pleasure is mine, Paige."

When his eyes meet mine, holding my gaze, I do my best not to flinch.

"Such a beauty," he says in a breath, his expression rapt. "With eyes like the stars and a power so fierce it burns just as hot. It's no wonder you've bewitched my brother. Pray tell, my pet, what is your power?"

"Dantalion," Kincaid growls, and his brother gives pause before the light is back in his eyes.

"Very well," Dantalion says with a mischievous smirk pulling at one corner of his mouth. "Keep your secrets, brother, but I would have a dance with the lovely lady—if she'll allow?"

With a glance between Kincaid and Dantalion, my stomach plummets to my toes. "I—"

"Lovely," Dantalion interrupts, pulling me toward the dance.

Tori watches me go with a raised brow and a little

waggle of her fingers. "You kids have fun," she calls after us.

When I turn to Kincaid, my throat goes dry. He watches us go in unconcealed rage. The tips of his horns push out through the artful arrangement of his black hair. His fists are black as a starless night sky, the color-absorbing shade coiling upward over his forearms.

I'm about to tell him I'll be right back when Dantalion tugs sharply on my hand and I'm drawn hard against him as the band begins a new song. It has a faster beat, and the courtiers watching the dance clap in sync every six notes.

Dantalion grins wickedly down on me as he moves me over the floor. I barely keep up, my feet sloppy and my form a mess. But he doesn't seem to mind. With one hand held tight against my lower back and my right hand clasped tightly in his, he guides me through spins and dips. Through quick steps forward and back and then forward again.

The dance goes on until I am breathless, and I'm certain my face is flushed, and just when I think if he spins me one more time I might fall on my face, the song slows and moves into another. This one slower.

I try to pull away, but the golden-haired lord doesn't release me. His hand on my lower back draws me nearer instead, bringing my body against his. I can't help noticing how he smells of bergamot and clean linen.

"So, my pet, won't you tell me what it is you're doing here with my brother?"

My mind seems to sway with my body as Dantalion moves us through the other dancers. I try not to pay any attention to the fact that they are all staring openly at us, making no secret of their surprise or their distaste.

"He made me come," I say and then immediately bite my tongue.

"Ah," says Dantalion, seemingly pleased with that response. "Not here of your own volition then?"

"No. Well, actually, I suppose I did want to come."

What the fuck, Paige? I can't seem to stop myself from answering him. Each time I try to concoct a response, my mouth betrays my intentions and blurts the first thing that pops into it.

Dantalion leans in close to my side. His lips are a whisper against my cheek. "Of course, you did," he says into my ear, eliciting a shiver. "And what exactly is it that my brother wants with you?"

I keep my teeth pressed hard against my tongue. Hard enough that the coppery tang of blood seeps into my mouth and I choke on it. But the words are like a weed growing strong and swift from my windpipe. Soon, I can't keep them from tumbling out.

"To find out what I am," I say, breathless.

I catch a glimpse of Kincaid at the edge of the room as Dantalion twirls me in a lazy circle and draws me back into his hard chest. "Is that so?"

"Yes."

"*Very* interesting."

"Please," I say through gritted teeth and swallow hard to quell the rise of bile in my stomach. I don't know what he's doing to me or how he's doing it, but I need him to stop. "I don't want to dance anymore."

Dantalion pouts. "Is it that you wish I were another partner, my pet?"

In the blink of an eye, Dantalion's angelic visage shifts and I am left staring into the yellow-eyed gaze of Kincaid. His long fingers clasp mine tightly. His scent fills my nose.

A shriek builds in my chest, and I try again to pull away, but Kincaid holds fast.

"Enough." The growl comes from behind me, and when finally Dantalion's grip is loosened, I stagger back and rough hands steady me with an iron grip on my waist before I can fall.

The Kincaid behind me glares at the Kincaid I just danced with, and I begin to feel light-headed. This isn't real.

This isn't happening.

The Kincaid in front of me clasps a hand to his belly in a deep bellowing laugh. He bends to the force of it, and when he raises his head, the laughter changes to a pitchy chortle and Dantalion's face stares back at me, tears blurring his sapphire eyes.

"Oh, I need to get myself one of those," Dantalion says between fits of laughter, wiping a finger beneath his eye to flick away a tear. "Where did you find it, brother?"

"That's *enough* Dantalion," Kincaid hisses, pulling me to his side. "You've had your fun. I think it's time you took your leave."

All traces of laughter leave the other demon lord's face. As he quiets, so does the room. Dancers pause and gape. The band ceases playing.

In their eyes, I see a wild excitement. A thirst to witness bloodshed.

In place of Dantalion's easy smile comes a sneer strong enough to make the blood curdle and clot in my veins.

His blue eyes darken until they're black from edge to edge.

"I think I'll decide when I'm ready to take my leave, *brother*."

Dantalion straightens his jacket and lifts his chin. He waves an arm toward the band and shouts, *"Music!"* before he rips a Diablim woman dressed in gold from her startled partner and begins to dance once more.

"He asked me things," I say as Kincaid slowly walks me back to the edge of the room. "And I couldn't stop myself from answering him."

"Dantalion has a power over one's deepest secrets and desires. He draws them out like blood from a wound. And, if you hadn't noticed, he can also take on the face of any he chooses. Though he's quite fond of using mine."

He says that last part with a sourness puckering his mouth, and when I do not reply, he looks down on me with a tenderness I didn't know he possessed.

Kincaid brushes a stray hair back from my cheek, and his gaze hardens. "I think it's time for us to leave."

27

The sea of courtiers parts for us as we make our exit. Only one rushes to catch up. Tori. She pouts as we walk along beside the food-laden tables. "You just arrived," she whines. "And the only other person who'll speak to me is Tristane, and you know how I loathe that angelic bastard."

"He's here?"

"Of course, he is. With that awful wench he brought the last time. *Isolde.*"

"When you say angelic, do you mean Nephilim?" I ask, trying to crane my neck to see back into the grand ballroom, trying to spot a glowy aura like Artemis'. Some of the Diablim have a faint light around them if I let my eyes go a little unfocused but none shine like Artemis.

"Isolde, yes. But the douche canoe Tristane is all

angel, baby. Pretty as you please but with a temper like a bloody hellhound."

"Watch yourself," Kincaid whispers harshly to Tori, pausing in his quick steps to face her. "You shouldn't say such things. You know why he's here. Why he comes. He could have you tossed into the pit in the blink of an eye, Tori. Don't be so cocky."

Tori's violet eyes narrow as she smirks. "Good thing I've got a get-out-of-Hell-free-card, am I right?"

Kincaid rolls his eyes.

"*Goodnight,* Tori."

"Fine! Ruin all my fun."

She waves at me as Kincaid pulls us back into a quick walk down the star-dappled black carpet and toward the already waiting gangstermobile idling at the end.

I'm surprised the door isn't pried from its hinges when Kincaid wrenches it open and corrals me into the backseat. I wince when my backside connects with something solid on the seat and squirm to get Kincaid's hooked staff out from under me.

A scream echoes from within the Midnight Court, and all heads swivel to find the source. Kincaid stills outside the door.

"What was th—"

Kincaid hushes me, and I go silent and still, straining to hear what he's hearing.

All conversation from the few Diablim milling about the open air outside the court ceases. It makes it easier to hear when the scream comes again, this time joined by several others.

I think I hear Tori among them.

"Kincaid?" I urge, my heart in my throat. "What's going on?"

His teeth bared and horns curling out from his skull, Kincaid snatches the hooked staff from my fingertips and turns his burning gaze to me for the briefest second.

"Stay here," he commands and then slams the door, sealing off the bulk of the hair-raising sounds as I watch him move in a blur of black back inside.

The crush of bodies rushing to follow him back in blots him out until I can't see him at all anymore.

My hands are cold and slick with clammy sweat as I fumble with the door handle until I've spilled back onto the black carpet. The chill in the air feels icier than it did only a minute before, and I hike up the hem of my dress to keep from tripping and kick off the obnoxious shoes.

My circlet falls askew as I shoulder through the crush of Diablim angling for a better view of the ballroom.

I hear them whisper. Hear them shout.

"What's happening to him?" They cry.

"Someone help him!"

But they are mere background noise to the rush of blood in my ears and the song of adrenaline spurring my heart to racing.

"Paige!" Tori's voice breaks through the din, and I find her violet eyes just as she reaches me, her hands clasping mine.

"What's happening?" I demand, trying to see over the last few heads blocking my view of the main chamber.

They part enough for me to see within just as Tori says, "It's Dantalion."

The golden-haired lord is on his knees at the center of the great hall. The courtiers have given him a wide berth—they ring the walls, watching in horror and awe as he clutches his chest, a pained growl passing through his bared teeth.

Kincaid kneels at his side, shouting something I can't hear over all the whispering, shouting voices. His staff, glowing a faint blue beneath the black casing, is discarded beside Dantalion.

"What's happening to him?"

Tori shakes her head. "I don't know," she tells me. "He was fine one minute and then he just...just *dropped*."

An agonizing howl peals from Dantalion's lips. His black eyes bulge as Kincaid shakes him.

"Poison?" I hear someone ask behind me and another Diablim replies with a sneer.

"Poison? You really think a lord of Hell can be undone with *poison*? Are you daft?"

But that is exactly what it looks like. My stomach turns at the paleness of his flesh. The red veins spidering out from his eyes like creeping vines over his face. The froth on his lips.

Until it all stops.

Time stops.

The room holds a collective breath as Dantalion croaks his last. The instant his face goes slack, he bursts into a billow of dark smoke and dissipates into the air.

Gone.

Just...*gone*.

Kincaid is left clutching empty air as the courtiers look on with wide eyes and even wider mouths.

"Impossible," one says while several others demand to know where Dantalion has gone. I'm not listening to them, though, not really. My gaze remains fixed on the spot where Dantalion had just been because they shout and scream that he's gone, and he was, for a second.

Now, Dantalion stands in horror before Kincaid, his sapphire eyes looking down where he was a second before. He stares at his hands as though the lines in his palms hold all the secrets of the universe, and then, as though he can feel my eyes on him, he lifts his head and stares straight into me.

His mouth opens, but no sound comes from him. Dantalion roars his fury in hollow silence until even the ghost of him is gone and I'm left blinking into the space where he just stood.

"Paige?" Tori urges, tugging on my arm. "Are you all right? You look like—"

Kincaid goes for his staff just as the inky black shadow of his demon form finishes creeping over his cheek. His already muscled body strains against the bonds of his tailored jacket, tearing at the seams. His pants shred to ribbons and a barbed tail sweeps low over the marble floor as he lifts his staff.

I shove past Tori and shoulder through the last few bodies between me and Kincaid.

"Wait," I shout, but he's beyond hearing me. "Kincaid, *wait*!"

I don't know why, but everything in my body is screaming that he isn't safe. I have this terrible feeling that if he leaves, he may not ever come back.

That's two demon lords now. Malphas *and* Dantalion.

Two unkillable demons are dead.

And Kincaid is about to rush into the fires of Hell to search for them.

He needs to know he won't find them there. He needs to stay.

"He's gone," I say, clearing the gap as Kincaid lifts his staff and slams it into the marble.

Cracks form in the stone, snaking out from his strike.

I barrel into his side at the same moment the staff strikes the marble for the second time and both of us spiral down into the dark.

. . .

A SCREAM IS YANKED FROM MY LUNGS AND MY BODY bends and twists under the pressure of whatever dark magic Kincaid is using. His hands are securely around me, holding me together. Keeping me from falling apart. From being obliterated. I can see nothing in the dark save for the glow of two wide yellow eyes. I can feel nothing but pain, Kincaid's rough hands, and the soft touch of smoke on my cheeks.

It's over in mere seconds, and I am on my knees against hard stone. The repulsive smell of sulfur assaults my nose, and a blistering heat ripples over me, wringing sweat from every pore.

A myriad of barbaric sounds filter through the deafening roar of a raging fire.

I choke and sputter, trying to catch my breath as my bones sing in agony. They feel as though they've each been bent to the point of snapping, but none have broken.

"Paige," Kincaid growls, and I can feel his hands on my back. I shy away from his touch, my skin sensitive and raw, like I lost a few layers of it on the way down.

On the way down...

Oh fuck.

With a groan, I force my eyes to open, and then I gasp.

We're high off the ground, standing at the top of a tall gray stone tower. Beyond the battlements is a scene unlike any to be found on earth, cementing my fear.

"No," I hear myself whisper, tears springing to my

eyes though I can't be sure whether they're from the oppressive heat or from what they've now been forced to see.

Those barbaric sounds weren't just the howling of the wind through the raging flames.

They are screams.

They are growls and snarls and the flapping of great black wings.

In the distance, amid a landscape charred to bitter black ash, is a funnel of flame shot down from the sunless sky to reach the blackened wreckage of the ground.

Within the swirl of fire, naked bodies fall screaming into the bowels of Hell. Great black winged beasts watch their descent, flying over a congregation of screaming demons jeering and shouting as more and more mortal souls fall to join them for an eternity of torment.

Ever since Lucifer walked the earth, we knew Hell had to be real. Where else would he have come from? Where did the Diablim and Nephilim come from if Heaven and Hell did not exist?

But knowing it and seeing it are two impossibly different things.

"K-Kincaid," I manage through the blockage in my throat, pushing myself to stand despite the pain.

Gently, he brushes a hand down my arm and takes my hand, tugging me to him. When finally I am able to tear my gaze away from the flaming cyclone and back to him, I see that he isn't the Kincaid who danced with me at the Midnight Court.

Nor the Kincaid I kissed in a darkened corridor below it.

He's in his demon form, with skin black as the ash floating around us like morbid snow. His horns glimmer in the orange glow of the flames in the distance and his yellow eyes burn.

"Do not fear me, *Na'vazēm.*"

"This is Hell, isn't it?"

He nods gravely. "You shouldn't have tried to stop me."

"Please." I choke, a fresh wave of hot tears welling in my eyes. "Take me back."

His lips press into a tight line. "No one except for the seven lords can leave Hell, Paige," he tells me, brushing the sweat-dampened hair from my eyes.

My bottom lip trembles, and I stumble back from him, shaking my head.

"*No,*" I say in a breath, every inch of me shaking like a leaf in the wind. If my heart were beating any faster, it would beat straight through my breast-bone.

A wave of vertigo almost takes me back to my knees, but I fight it, pressing the half-moons of my nails in my palms. "No," I repeat, more firmly this time. "You take me back, Kincaid."

"I can't."

"Yes, you can. You promised Tori…"

"I lied."

My heart stops.

"There's only one way out—a gauntlet. I promised Tori she would have her chance at freedom, but no more. She will have the opportunity to run the gauntlet should she ever need it, but only one soul has ever made it to its end."

A scorching fury explodes in my belly, and without thinking, I shove Kincaid hard in the chest. "Fuck that," I bite out. "Tap your stupid staff thingy and *take me back*."

The blue light shimmers beneath its black surface, pulsing with latent power. If he won't take me, I'm ready to make a grab for the thing and do it myself.

"You can't travel by the staff, *Na'vazēm*. It isn't—"

He cuts himself off and then without preamble closes the short gap between us and presses his hand to my chest. His wild yellow eyes widen and then narrow, meeting mine.

I shuck off his hand and glare at him. "What?" I demand.

"You should be dead."

He rubs a wide hand over his face, and I notice how some of the black shadow beneath his flesh is seeping away, slowly changing him back to the Kincaid I recognize.

"Your heart still beats, *Na'vazēm*."

He grips me by the shoulders, and his face splinters into agonizing relief. "It should have killed you. Your soul should belong to *him*."

He presses his hand to my chest again and barks a bewildered laugh. "I can save you," he says and wraps me into his hickory-and-musk scented embrace. "I can save you."

His staff taps against the gray stone once. I gasp, rushing to knot my hands into the tattered remains of his jacket. Twice and I brace myself for the long fall.

"Hold on," he whispers into my ear, and the floor vanishes from beneath our feet, Hell along with it.

❧ 28 ❧

The instant we're back on solid ground, I have to rip myself from Kincaid to retch onto the polished marble. My body heaves until there's nothing left.

Vaguely, I can hear a familiar voice calling to me, but it's like I'm hearing it under water. Dampening the voice are new screams.

Not the pained screams of the damned, but the surprised shouts of the courtiers still ringing the spot where Dantalion vanished in the Midnight Court.

I want to smack Kincaid for bringing us back here. Why didn't he just transport us back to the damn house?

I shiver against a biting chill. My Hell-warmed flesh steams in the earthen air.

The voices come clearer once I am able to draw a

full breath. I wince when Kincaid lifts me from the floor and steadies me with an arm barred across my middle. "I have to go back," he's saying. "I need you to take her to the house and stay with her."

"I can do that," the familiar voice replies, and I'm passed from Kincaid to Tori. Her hands are cool on my scalded skin, and when I shiver, she pulls me to her, wrapping something thick and warm around my shoulders.

In a daze, I remember what I needed to tell Kincaid —why this all happened. "Wait," I implore him in a croak, reaching out a hand to grab his wrist. I blink through the grainy haze clouding my vision to meet his eyes. "Dantalion is dead."

I feel him stiffen beneath my fingers.

"How do you know?"

I swallow past the razorblades in my throat and give his wrist what I hope is a comforting squeeze. From what I could tell, Dantalion was a total dick, but he was still Kincaid's brother.

"Because I saw his spirit."

Kincaid yanks his arm away before I can even finish, and Tori catches me before I can trip forward.

"You're wrong," he growls, eyes ablaze.

"No," I say, exuding confidence I don't fully feel. "I don't think I am."

Kincaid looks past me to Tori and the black coat of his demon form creeps back over his skin. *"Take her home."*

He taps his staff twice on the marble floor and vanishes in a coil of black smoke. My chest aches anew at his absence and that same feeling—the one that tries to tell me he's in danger—returns with a vengeance. Except now, I can't help him.

As the smoke dissipates, I catch the eye of a man across the room. He stands with arms crossed over a wide chest. His skin is radiant gold. His hair is polished copper. Though he has one of the most beautiful faces I think I've ever seen, the way he has it twisted makes me cower against Tori.

His silvery gray eyes burrow into me like arrowheads shot from a bow.

That's when I notice the strange band of light over his head.

Like a ring of white fire or a perfect circle of incense smoke.

It's...a halo, I realize.

"Come on," Tori tells me, and we begin to move through the courtiers. The angel is lost as Diablim close in all around us.

They reach out to me with clawed hands and reverence in their red eyes.

"Impossible," they whisper as we pass.

"A miracle," some shout over the din of incoherent chatter.

"Don't touch her," Tori snarls at them as we go. "Get *back*."

The crisp night air is a welcome balm to my nerves

as we break through the crush of perfumed bodies and out onto the black carpet. Tori drags me to its edge just as Kincaid's black town car pulls up, like the driver somehow knew we were coming.

Tori helps me inside and then slides in next to me, slamming the door behind her. "Drive," she orders the man in the front seat. "Don't stop for anything."

She turns on me the instant the car veers onto the road. "Who the hell are you?" she demands. "*What* are you?"

My eyes sting again, and I try to erect a dam against the swell of tears in my chest, but it's no use. I shake my head. "I don't know."

Tori's vibrant violet eyes soften, and she tugs the cloak across my shoulders more tightly closed. She places a hand over mine on the seat. "I'm sorry," she says. "It's going to be all right."

Is it?

Then why do I feel like nothing is ever going to be all right again?

"He'll come back, right?"

Tori cocks her head at me and understanding widens her eyes almost imperceptibly. She nods once.

"Yes," she says, and the certainty in her tone lessens the weight on my chest enough that I finally feel like I can breathe. "He always comes back."

I sigh, allowing her words to cocoon me in their warm embrace. After a few moments, I'm able to blunt the sharp edge of panic making my hands tremble. After a few moments more, I sit straighter.

Tori presses a chilled metal flask into my hand and curls my fingers around it. "Have some," she says and leans back in her seat. "You need it more than I do."

I take a long swallow of the nectar-like liquor, grimacing as it pools in my belly like acid. But she's right, it does take some of the edge off.

He always comes back.

"*So*," Tori says after the silence has stretched on between us.

"So?"

I hand the flask back to her.

"Are we going to talk about the fact that you've just been to Hell and back, or…?"

I blink at her and suddenly, what remains of the sulfuric smell in my nose is overpowering, and I can still feel the flush of hellfire on my cheeks.

"I mean, what was it like?"

I snatch the flask back for another swig and look away. "Trust me, Tori," I tell her. "You don't want to know."

Follow the story of Paige and Kincaid in SINS OF THE DAMNED, *Fallen Cities: Elisium book two! Get it here: https://mybook.to/sotd*

BONUS

Read an exclusive bonus chapter from Kincaid's point of view by joining Elena Lawson's fan group or subscribing to her newsletter!

ABOUT THE AUTHOR

ELENA LAWSON writes paranormal and fantasy stories full of feisty heroines, unforgettable heroes, and spellbinding romance. When she comes out of her writing cave, she can be found obsessively rearranging her bookshelves, binge-watching her favorite shows, or cooking overly fancy meals for her family and friends. Elena can be found online at www.elenalawson.com

Made in United States
North Haven, CT
03 May 2023

36187924R00171